Charming But INSANE

Charming But Insane

SUE LIMB

BLOOMSBURY

LONDON BERLIN NEW YORK SYDNEY

Bloomsbury Publishing, London, Berlin, New York and Sydney

First published in Great Britain in 2004 by Bloomsbury Publishing Plc
50 Bedford Square, London, WC1B 3DP

This revised edition first published in January 2012

Text copyright © Sue Limb 2004
Revised text copyright © Sue Limb 2012

A CIP catalogue record for this book is available from the British Library

ISBN 978 1 4088 1726 1

Typeset by Hewer Text UK Ltd, Edinburgh
Printed in Great Britain by Clays Ltd, St Ives plc, Bungay, Suffolk

1 3 5 7 9 10 8 6 4 2

www.bloomsbury.com
www.JessJordan.co.uk

For
and, to be honest,
to a certain extent actually
by
Betsy Vriend

Chapter 1

Eyes, nose, lips. Jess was drawing a face on her hand. She should have been making notes for her history essay: a list of 'Reasons Why King Charles I Was Unpopular'. But instead she was giving herself a love-tattoo of the beautiful Ben Jones. The flicked-up hair, the slanty grin . . . Oh no! It didn't look like Ben Jones at all. It looked like a demented iguana.

Art wasn't Jess's strong point. She wrote, *Ben Jones, – or Demented Iguana?* under her tattoo, and coughed in a signal to her friend Flora that communication was desired. It was a kind of ringtone. Flora looked up and Jess held the tattoo up to her. Flora smiled, but it was a kind of pretend smile, and immediately afterwards Flora glanced furtively at Miss Dingle and dived straight back into her work.

Miss Dingle – Dingbat to her fans – was glaring

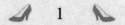

from the teacher's desk. 'Jess Jordan! What's your problem?'

'Oh, Miss, there are so many,' sighed Jess, hastily pulling her sleeve down to hide the portrait-tattoo of Ben Jones: the Demented Iguana. 'Tragic broken home, hideous genetic inheritance . . . massive bum . . .' A few people giggled.

'Get on with your work,' snapped Miss Dingle, trying to sound steely and terrifying, even though she had a weedy little voice and a tendency to spit. 'If you showed half as much interest in writing history projects as you do in trying to be amusing, you'd be the star pupil instead of the class dunce.'

Everybody hid their faces in their books and cracked up – as silently as possible, of course. The whole room shook.

'And the rest of you!' shouted Miss Dingle. 'Be quiet and get on with writing your list of reasons – unless you all want to stay behind after school! I'm quite tempted to put the whole group in detention!' At the word 'detention', another drop of spit went sailing across the room.

There was a muffled explosion as everyone tried to avoid laughing out loud by eating their own tonsils, but frenzied scribbling was also resumed. Nobody wanted to stay behind after school. Jess picked up her dictionary and tried to look intelligent. She turned the pages, hoping for a rude word. Suddenly she had an idea. Hey! Maybe you could consult the dictionary, a bit like the Tarot. Think of a question, then open it at random. Jess closed her eyes and concentrated. *Will Ben Jones and I ever be an item?*

Her finger jabbed at a word. *Parsley. A well-known garden herb, used for flavouring soup.* Well, not a brilliant result, obviously. But maybe there was a hidden meaning. Perhaps you could make a boy fall in love with you by rubbing parsley behind your ears, or sprinkling chopped parsley in his pants while he was swimming.

Jess suddenly caught Dingbat's eye again. A dangerous moment. Hastily Jess copied down the title of the history essay. 'Reasons Why King Charles I Was Unpopular.' All she had to do was read chapter six of the history book. Jess flicked through the book and looked at the pictures. Charles I had sad, haunted eyes and a stylish goatee. Flora had told her that he had been only about five feet tall. Some kind of Hobbit, obviously. And then he had had his head chopped off – pretty bad news for anybody of course, but for a short guy clearly a disaster, stylewise.

'Reasons Why King Charles I Was Unpopular.' Jess looked across at Flora, who was writing so hard that her whole body was shaking. She had written three whole pages already, and if Jess was going to catch up with her, she had to make a start. Jess picked up her pen and let her imagination run away with her. This was always dangerous.

Reasons Why King Charles I Was Unpopular
1. He never changed his pants.
2. He refused to grow.
3. He passed a law saying everybody taller than him had to have their legs cut off.
4. He slurped his soup.
5. He used to bottle his farts and sell them to the tourists.

Somehow, at this point, Jess's inspiration dried up and she began to think about Ben Jones again. She formed a plan to steal a bit of DNA from his football boots or a hair from the shoulder of his blazer. There would be instructions somewhere on the internet, so she ought to be able to genetically engineer a Ben Jones look-alike, in case the real one proved unavailable. She gazed in adoration at the tattoo of Ben Jones: the

Demented Iguana. How she longed to have his babies. Or possibly lay his eggs.

Jess started another list: 'Reasons Why Ben Jones Is Popular.' This was much easier than the history list.

1. Hair like golden grass (if only I could picnic on it).
2. Eyes blue enough to swim in (he's beginning to sound like a holiday destination).
3. A cute, slow, slanty smile that could defrost Antarctica.
4. Doesn't speak much, i.e. not loud and trashy, and . . .
5. Oozes mystery and charisma.

Suddenly, the bell rang. A massive sigh of relief spread through the room. Everybody put down their pens, yawned and stretched. Tiffany, a plump, dark-haired girl with savage eyebrows, turned round to Jess and hissed, 'Don't forget my party tomorrow night! Be there or else!'

'Sure,' said Jess. 'I was gonna stay in and darn some divine socks, but for you – I'll make that major sacrifice.' Tiffany's family was quite rich – at least, by Jess's standards – and Jess was quite looking forward to quaffing champagne and swinging from the chandeliers.

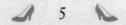

Jess's best friend, the goddess Flora, was the only person in the class who hadn't finished working yet. She scribbled away harder than ever, her golden hair glittering. One grain of her divine dandruff could make the blind see again, and revive small insects that had been trodden on.

Flora finished off her sentence with a flourish, tossed back her hair with a great flash of supernatural light, turned to Jess and grinned. *It's a good job the beautiful, over-achieving glamour puss is my best friend*, thought Jess, *or I might just have to kill her*.

'Jess Jordan!' thundered Miss Dingle in her tiny fairy's voice, above the noise of people packing up their bags. 'Will you come up here and show me your list of reasons, please!'

Chapter 2

Detention was quite relaxing, actually. Jess wrote her extra work in very large handwriting and managed to cover five pages. Miss Dingle seemed preoccupied. She kept writing things down and then screwing up pieces of paper and throwing them away. Maybe she was drafting a Lonely Hearts ad.

History teacher, 38 but looks 57, bad hair, flat chest, knock knees, tendency to spit, seeks gentleman companion with reliable umbrella for badminton and what follows naturally.

Although Jess's own Lonely Hearts ad wouldn't be very tempting either.

Girl, 15, charming but insane, huge bum, massive ears, seeks . . . Well, seeks Ben Jones, but failing that, a pantomime-horse costume to cover her deformities.

Jess handed her essay in. Miss Dingbat made a long sad speech about how clever Jess was, how well she could do if she tried and how terribly she was under-achieving. All her teachers were desperately upset about it. Jess imagined them all weeping in the staffroom. There had never been under-achievement like it, apparently. It was almost an achievement in itself. *A shame there isn't a prize for under-achievement*, thought Jess. *I'd walk it.*

'Now, Jess,' tinkled Dingbat with a severe frown, 'underneath all your wise-cracking I know there's a serious scholar trying to get out. Think how proud your parents would be if you realised your potential. Now off you go – and remember, I'll be looking for signs of improvement!'

Jess nodded, trying to look tragic and guilty, and left the classroom.

She started thinking about her dad. If only he lived nearby! Two hundred miles is a long way to walk if you want to drop round after school. Her dad sent her silly text messages and joke 'horrorscopes' every day. But she hadn't seen him face to face for months.

Jess's mum and dad had separated soon after she was born, possibly because of the shock of her appearance. Judging by the baby photos, she had resembled a bald and poisonous pudding. Perhaps they had blamed each other. Anyway, soon afterwards her dad had gone off to live in Cornwall, which is about as far away as you can get without actually entering the sea.

Fred Parsons was sitting on the wall outside school. He had his hood up and his big grey eyes looked out from under it like an owl in a cave. Jess pulled his hood off. Fred had long wispy hair which hung down messily around his collar. Only people with thick hair should grow it long. But Fred cultivated the eccentric Victorian poet hairdo because he thought it made him look like an intellectual.

'Get your blinking hair cut!' boomed Jess, like an army sergeant. She always greeted Fred this way. 'Get off that wall, stand tall, eyes on the horizon! You look like the Hunchback of Notre Dame.'

'Ah, Miss Jess Jordan!' Fred greeted her, ripping out his earphones. 'How was detention? Pleasant, I hope? Did Dingbat shower you with saliva?'

'We bonded quite nicely, thank you,' replied Jess. I helped her draft her Lonely Hearts ad. We are now the best of friends. Practically inseparable.'

'I wasn't waiting for you, by the way,' said Fred. 'I was merely too tired to walk home after school. I might even not go home at all and sleep here. It'll save time in the morning.'

Jess knew he had waited for her, though. They always walked home together. She had known Fred since they were three years old. They had met at play-group, when he had hit her over the head with an inflatable bus.

'I was thinking of calling at Flora's on the way home,' said Jess. 'Wanna come?'

Fred got up off the wall and they set off together. 'I'm not coming in when we get to her place,' he said. 'I will never enter the Barclay household. I'd rather see my mother dance naked in front of the whole school.'

OK, Flora's house was a bit intimidating. It was rather like heaven. Flora and her sisters, Freya and Felicity, were all blonde. Her mother was blonde. Her dad was blond. The dog was blond. Even the carpets were blond. You had to take your shoes off by the front door and walk about in your socks.

After about ten minutes they reached Flora's. It was a tall, elegant building painted white, with neatly-clipped bushes in chic pots either side of the front steps. Somehow the birds never pooed on Flora's house. It was a sign that the Barclay family were the Chosen Ones. Things were very different at Jess's ramshackle little home, two streets away. Stray dogs travelled miles across the city and queued up to poo in her front garden.

'Come in with me, Fred!' whispered Jess. 'Flora's dad is so scary. Please. Just for a minute. You can engage him in masculine talk about cars or football or something. You only have to take your shoes off. You won't have to be disinfected or anything.'

Fred backed off. 'I would rather have all the hairs in my nostrils pulled out one by one than spend half a minute in that hell-hole. Besides, my socks smell of an expensive French cheese that has been left out in the sun.'

Jess stood stranded on the doorstep. Fred retreated up the road. Jess frantically tried to think of something to say that would detain him.

'Wait! Wait! What are you going to do tomorrow night? There's a party at Tiffany's. Are you coming?'

'No way!' Fred pulled a face. 'I plan to lie down

on the sofa and watch something very violent on TV.'

Jess felt disappointed. Fred was so NOT a party animal. She sighed and rang Flora's bell. Fred slouched off down the road in the manner of an orang-utan. When he got to the corner, he looked back, and Jess stuck out her lip, scratched her armpits and made a hooting noise like a chimpanzee. It was at this moment that Flora's dad opened the door.

Flora's dad made Jess uneasy. He was tall, jovial and terrifying. Everybody was afraid of him. His wife. His daughters. His dog. Even his carpet.

'Shoes off, please, Jess!' he commanded. 'How was extra French?'

'Extra French?' stuttered Jess. Flora appeared behind her dad, gesturing frenziedly. 'Oh, it was fine.' Jess tried to think of the French for 'fine'. '*Très belle.*'

Too late, she realised that meant 'very beautiful'. But Flora's dad didn't seem to care.

'You must excuse me,' he said. 'I'm ordering some bidets from Turin.'

He went back to the telephone and started talking in Italian, complete with gestures, which Jess thought was a little unnecessary. What a show-off! At least her own dad kept a low profile. The most assertive thing he had ever done was to send her a small sketch of a seagull. She would have preferred banknotes, obviously, but at least she could say her dad was a romantic artist starving in St Ives.

'Come in, Jess!' called Flora's mum.

Jess and Flora went into the sitting room. 'I told them you were at extra French,' whispered Flora, 'so they won't think you're a bad influence.'

'Jess! How lovely to see you!' Flora's mother was sprawled on the sofa, wearing an oyster-coloured satin dressing-gown like a glamorous movie star from the 1930s. She was drying her nail varnish by blowing on it through big, pink lips.

'Do excuse the mess,' said Mrs Barclay. Jess looked around in vain for a mess. The Barclay family didn't know the meaning of the word. If there was an Olympic event called 'Making a Mess', Flora's family would have to train arduously for months just to master the basics. Even then they'd probably think Making a Mess involved Not Rinsing Your Toothbrush.

'Excuse my *déshabille*,' said Flora's mother. Jess supposed that was a reference to the dressing-gown. If only she really *had* done extra French. 'I've just had a bath, and Henry and I are going to the opera. You must be tired after all that extra French. Get poor Jess a hot chocolate with cream, Flora. Sit down by me, Jess darling, and relax. Would you like a sandwich? How's your mother?'

'Oh, fine, thanks.' Jess wanted to say as little as possible about her mother.

'I saw her in the library yesterday,' drawled Mrs Barclay, inspecting her manicured nails with satisfaction. 'I was terrified because I was late with my whodunnits, but she was very kind and forgave me.'

Jess smiled gratefully. It was awful having a mother who worked in the library. Everybody saw her in her sad shoes, nerdy glasses and dreadful old hippie clothing. Sometimes she even forgot to comb her hair. How wonderful it would be to have a mother like Flora's, who called you 'darling'. Jess's mother only called her 'darling' when she was about to break some bad news, or apologise for a major failure on the maternal front.

It would also be wonderful to have sisters. Freya, Flora's elder sister, was away at Oxford University studying maths and How to Be a Love Goddess (the family business). Felicity, the youngest, was a musical genius. She played the flute. Jess could hear her tootling away even now, up in her bedroom. Felicity also kept doves in a dovecote out in the garden, and they flew to her windowsill and received tasty dove-food from her perfect white hands. Jess had no sisters or brothers, just a threadbare old teddy bear called Rasputin.

Flora's mum and dad went off to get dressed for their night out, and Flora made a cream cheese and gherkin sandwich for Jess. It was her favourite snack. Flora often prepared delicious treats for her. Sometimes it seemed she got more mothering from Flora than she did from her actual mum.

'I'm so in love with King Charles I!' sighed Flora.

'Look, Flo, he's just not right for you,' said Jess. 'It's the age gap. He's three hundred years older than you. People will talk. Plus he has no head. And even if he did have one, he wouldn't even come up to your shoulder.'

'Such a tragic life, though,' said Flora. She was a sucker for a sob story. Eventually Jess persuaded her that, if they went to Tiffany's party, there might be a boy there who looked a bit like King Charles I. Or, failing that, at least one who had recently been beaten up or who was recovering from a dangerous illness.

The only problem now was what to wear. And they only had twenty-four hours to decide. They agreed to spend the next morning in the mall. The lack of suitable clothing was a crisis of truly global proportions. It required heroic action. So they decided to meet at ten o'clock in the morning – which, as far as Jess was concerned, was still the middle of the night.

Chapter 3

Jess's dad had texted her one of his 'horrorscopes'. But Jess wasn't worrying about the werewolf in the cupboard under the stairs. She had a more immediate problem: the size of her bum. She stared at herself in the huge mirrors of the communal changing room at Togs 'R' Us. She was wearing leopardskin stretch pants. Did her bum look big in this? You can bet your sweet life it did.

Geographically, Jess's backside was a mountain range. The sun rose over it – eventually. Huge birds of prey nested on its craggy heights and hunted in its shadows. It wouldn't have been so bad if Jess's bum were balanced by a nice big bosom. But geographically, Jess's boobs could not balance her bum at all. Her chest was the kind of featureless plain upon which airports are constructed.

If only, thought Jess, *some gifted cosmetic surgeon could slice off my bum and transplant it on to my chest, we'd be in business*. Then she would have a majestic cleavage. It was wasted out back, under her jeans. Oh well. They say a clever choice of clothes can conceal bad features and emphasise one's good points. But these leopardskin stretch pants weren't working. You don't see leopards waddling heavily across the plains, do you? They tend to streak across in a streamlined kind of way.

'Flora,' asked Jess, 'what's my best feature?'

Flora was admiring herself in a cute little black top. A pink navel-ring winked cheekily out above her grey hipsters. She looked divine. Flora's dad didn't know she'd had her navel pierced. If he ever found out, he would personally build a high stone tower and lock her up there until she was thirty. If that was what Having a Dad Around meant, you could keep it.

'Your best feature?' Flora hesitated.

Oh no! thought Jess. *She can't think of a single thing!*

'Your eyes are fantastic – and your neck – and your ears – and, well, you're fabulous all over, Jess. You're a babe.' Flora turned back with relief to the ravishing vision awaiting her in the mirror.

'But my bum is like some terrible gigantic Siamese

twin!' wailed Jess. 'It follows me around everywhere and gets stuck in doorways.'

'Your bum is great!' cried Flora, but her voice went up just a little too high. 'I wish I had a proper bum. I look like a boy.' Needless to say, Flora looked as much like a boy as a box of chocolates looks like a side of beef. Jess sighed.

Three hours later, having tried on approximately three thousand garments, Jess decided on a black top with a plunging neckline and a strange shawl-like black skirt.

'Boho!' said Flora approvingly. 'You look stunning, babe! Ben Jones will see you as he's never seen you before! Suddenly across a crowded room he will feel Cupid's dart!' They'd been doing all about Cupid in English with Mr Fothergill. They'd both tried to develop crushes on Mr Fothergill, but he simply was too fat and sweaty. You could more easily fancy a hippo.

Jess doubted if Ben Jones would fancy her, despite the plunging neckline and boho skirt. Life was so unfair. Everybody fancied Ben Jones, no matter what he wore. Although Flora said she preferred his best friend, Mackenzie, who was dark and rather short.

'It's a biology thing,' she explained. 'Blondes don't fancy blond guys. It's to avoid inbreeding.'

Jess was not completely convinced by this. After all, Flora's entire family was blond. Maybe Flora really fancied Ben Jones, but she was keeping quiet about it because Jess was so crazy about him. That would be a really loyal thing for a friend to do. But also, somehow, really annoying. If Flora did fancy Ben Jones, it would make her rather tragic and picturesque, and she had far too much going for her already.

They parted and Jess went back home to get ready. How could Jess cram it all into six hours? Flora had gone back to her palace where her granny – possibly a close relative of the Queen – would be distributing bags of gold over tea and exquisite little cakes. Jess's house, of course, was empty except for dirty dishes. Her mother had gone off to demonstrate against the war. She did this every Saturday. There was usually a war to demonstrate against. Jess didn't mind really. It kept her mum out of trouble and out of the way and it was free. Just as long as she didn't ever end up on TV, dancing for peace. Naked. This was Jess's most nightmarish fantasy.

Having a mum who was often out on demos also permitted Jess to surf the internet unchallenged by cries of, 'Get off that thing now! We'll get a bill as long as my arm!' Jess did a search on lingerie. Soon she was in the slightly weird world of bra inserts – not just little cotton pads but, apparently, bags containing water or silicone gel.

'Curves' are made of a specially formulated silicone gel, enclosed in a sheer, skin-like polyurethane cover. This material was developed for space research and is extremely well tolerated by the skin.

Wait a minute! Space research? What would be the effect of nil gravity? Wouldn't your boobs fly off in different directions? Besides, Jess didn't like the concept of outer space. She liked to keep her feet firmly on the ground.

Thank goodness I'm an earth sign, thought Jess. Flora was an air sign, of course – kind of angelic and ethereal. Still, never mind air and earth. What Jess needed now was water. She raced to the kitchen and found a roll of those small plastic bags which mothers use to wrap up sandwiches. At least, mothers good enough to make sandwiches for their beloved children, unlike the mother in question, Madeleine Jordan, at present protesting against the war while her child starved helplessly at home.

Jess filled a small plastic bag with water, tied it up

tightly and secured it with a rubber band. It was quite gel-like. She wobbled it around in her hand. It did indeed move rather like breast tissue. She didn't have enough breast tissue of her own to have conducted personal research on the subject. But she had watched a lot of music videos.

She wasn't quite sure about the water, though. Perhaps a faint sloshing would be heard. And what if she sprang a leak? Jess shuddered at the thought of puddles on the floor. The jokes about potty-training would last a lifetime. Maybe there was a food substance a little less watery than water. Jess ransacked the food cupboard, and her eyes fell on a tin of soup. Minestrone!

Getting it into the bags was a little bit more laborious and messy, but fifteen minutes later, Jess had a cleavage. The bags of soup really worked. Amazing! She was going to have a ball! Now all she needed was a pumpkin coach or, failing that, the No. 109 bus, which would take her all the way to Tiffany's. She just had to spend four and a half hours on her eyebrows first.

Chapter 4

Seconds after arriving at Tiffany's, Jess was suddenly face to face with Ben Jones. He loomed up out of the crowd, looking gorgeous.

'Um . . . seen Mackenzie?' he said in that wonderfully slow drawl.

'No,' stammered Jess. 'I've only just arrived. Maybe he's . . .'

But Ben Jones had gone. He spoke slowly but he could move fast. And he hadn't even noticed her cleavage or her boho skirt. Mind you, it was very dark, and very crowded. Perhaps later there would be the magic moment, foretold by Flora, at which his eyes would find hers across a crowded room and he would suddenly realise . . . At least there was a crowded room, ready and waiting.

Tiffany lived in what used to be an old mansion

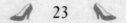

23

house which had been converted into flats. Her family's apartment covered most of the ground floor. Their sitting room was huge: half the size of the school gym. Tiffany's kitchen was amazing, with a high ceiling. Jess found Flora in there, surrounded by boys and picking daintily at a pizza. She was wearing diamanté strips across both her eyelids. Every time she blinked, there was a flash of rainbow light.

'Where on earth did you get those?' demanded Jess in amazement.

'My granny gave them to me!' said Flora. 'Aren't they amazing? But they make my eyelids feel sort of heavy. I think I shall have to go to bed in a minute.'

Nobody had even noticed Jess's cleavage. Jess didn't know whether to be pleased or furious. She decided it was just as well. She was beginning to smell of minestrone, which was unfortunate. She had doused herself in her mother's Calvin Klein. But the sweaty, soupy smell was winning. Jess was a bit worried. You shouldn't be able to smell the soup, surely, unless it had escaped somehow? She glanced down at her cleavage. Well, somebody had to. There was no sign of anything wrong.

Flora threw back her head and batted her diamanté

eyelashes at the ceiling. 'This is such an amazing kitchen!' she breathed. 'It must be really old. It's like a palace or something. You can imagine a princess sitting here after a night out at a ball, having a cup of hot chocolate and telling her butler all about it.' Jess sometimes suspected that in her most private dreams, Flora imagined she was a reincarnation of Princess Diana.

Tiffany's brother had the latest gothic video game and so the boys melted away.

'Do you believe in reincarnation?' pondered Jess.

'Oh, I don't know,' sighed Flora. 'Do you?'

'Yeah,' said Jess. 'I'm sure I had a previous life in ancient Egypt. As a dung beetle.'

'Oh, I so love ancient Egypt!' sighed Flora. 'I'd really like to have a black wig so I could go to parties as Cleopatra.'

This annoyed Jess slightly. She was supposed to be the dark one. Flora had the blonde beauty of a goddess in a painting. Wasn't that enough? At the very moment when Jess was poised to start hating Flora just a little bit, Flora slid off her chair and made Jess a cream cheese and gherkin sandwich.

'Notice anything different about me?' demanded Jess, halfway through the sandwich.

'Your hair! Your hair is great! How have you made it stick up like that?'

'No, not my hair, idiot.'

Flora's eyes ran up and down. 'Wow! Your tights! Fantastic! Fishnets are wicked! So Paris!'

'Not my tights, you fool!' yelled Jess. 'My cleavage!'

Flora inspected Jess's cleavage. 'It looks great!' she said. 'I don't know what you're so worried about! You've got a perfectly good cleavage! Look at it – it's fine!'

Jess felt deeply depressed. So Flora thought this was her very own cleavage. Suddenly she decided she wouldn't tell Flora about the bags of soup. It was just a little secret between herself and her boobs – which were called Bonnie and Clyde, incidentally.

Jess had got into the habit of talking to her boobs. 'Grow, you lazy so-and-so's!' That kind of thing. Only in private, though. Then it was just a short step to giving them names. Jess's mum didn't allow pets. The great advantage of boobs over dogs was that walkies didn't have to be a special expedition. Every time Jess went down to the corner shop for a new lipstick, Bonnie and Clyde got an outing.

And Jess's boobs were certainly getting their biggest

outing yet. Jess finished her sandwich, and she and Flora strolled into the main room, where deafening rap music was pouring out of Tiffany's enormous speakers. Ben Jones may not have noticed Jess's cleavage, even Flora may not have noticed, but Whizzer noticed right away.

Whizzer (William Izard to his family) was one of the boys a couple of years above Jess and Flora. He played football with a demonic energy. He had big, rather rude lips and a reputation for wicked ways. He appeared before Jess and rudely and wickedly interrupted her conversation with Flora by grabbing Jess's hand and pulling her into the dancing throng.

It was hardly the gracious invitation she would have preferred, but Jess began to go through her moves. As they gyrated and grooved, Whizzer fixed his eyes firmly on her cleavage. Jess began to wish she had worn a modest top which covered her up as far as – well, as far as her eyebrows. She wished she had at least rehearsed dancing before leaving home, in front of her full-length mirror. She feared that her newly-buoyant boobs might be getting rather out of hand. Bonnie especially – the left one – was beginning to feel a bit free-range, and it did seem a little draughty across her chest. Jess also began to worry that, in shaking up the soup so violently, she might somehow make it boil over.

Out of the corner of her eye she saw Flora smooching with Ben Jones's friend Mackenzie. Though short, Mackenzie was quite good-looking in a dark, poetic sort of way. In fact, he was probably the nearest thing to King Charles I available locally. Jess wasn't sure whether he had a sad and tormenting secret, but she was sure one could be arranged. It would be so cool if Flora could go out with Mackenzie and she could go out with Ben Jones. First, however, she had to get rid of Whizzer.

When the number ended, she tried to retreat gracefully back in the direction of the kitchen. Whizzer, however, pounced. He put his arms round her and stuck his tongue down her throat. Jess was disgusted. He tasted of cigarettes. And Ben Jones might be watching from somewhere nearby. She struggled slightly, trying to escape, but Whizzer squeezed her more tightly, and Bonnie – her left boob – exploded and a jet of minestrone soup shot up and hit him on the jaw. Whizzer let Jess go and staggered back, clawing at his soupy chin, cussing horribly. Jess seized her moment. She ran. Out in the hall, there was a bathroom. Somebody had put a sign saying 'Girlz' on the door.

The boys' toilet was marked 'Ladz' and was Tiffany's parents' en-suite.

Jess flew into 'Girlz' and slammed the bolt across. There was a loo, a washbasin and a wide shelf above it with a huge mirror. Tiffany had decorated it for the party with loads of leaves and flowers. But Jess didn't have time to admire the decor. She wriggled out of her plunging black top, and pulled the minestrone inserts out of her bra. The left-hand one had exploded all over Bonnie. Jess threw both bags of soup down the loo and flushed, then stripped to the waist and washed the chopped carrot and tomato and macaroni off her boobs.

'I'm sorry about this, Bonnie,' she apologised. 'But it's your own fault. If you and Clyde had just got your act together and grown a bit, I would never even have thought about inserts!'

Then she washed her bra, and put it back on. There are probably more uncomfortable feelings than climbing into a wet bra, but all the same, it was quite terrible. There was still soup in the loo. It looked as if somebody had vomitted. The thought was so sickening that, for an instant, Jess was on the edge of throwing up herself, but she pulled back just in time by imagining she was Christmas shopping in New York. Jess had never been to New York, but the shopping fantasy was a sure-fire cure for nausea. She closed her eyes and flushed the loo again.

Fully, if damply, dressed, she was now ready to leave. If there had been a window in the bathroom she would have climbed out of it, but at least when she left the bathroom she would already be in the hall, right by the front door. Her mascara was smudged. Never mind. In two seconds she would be out in the street. The lovely, dark, anonymous street.

Jess opened the door, shot out and almost collided with Ben Jones.

'Um, hi, Jess, I was looking for you . . .' he said, with a strange smile.

He knew! Everybody knew! News of her soup debacle was all over the county already!

'Sorry!' said Jess. 'I've got to go home, my mum just rang, she's not well.' She pushed past him – too upset even to enjoy the fleeting contact with his T-shirt – and rushed out into the street. He didn't follow, thank heavens. She wanted to be Home Alone as soon as possible. The bus stop for the 109 bus was too near Tiffany's house. Anyone could come out of the party and see her waiting there. Unfortunately, owing to a foolish desire to appear glamorous and cool, Jess had worn her mega-high heels, so she had to teeter in agony all the way home.

What a complete nightmare, thought Jess as she reached her own street. *How could things possibly get worse?*

Chapter 5

As Jess let herself in, she found her mum standing in the hall. She had a peculiar look on her face. Jess recognised that look. It was the same look as when her mum had broken Jess's porcelain doll by dropping a brass Buddha on it. Not deliberately, obviously. Jess's mum wasn't a sadist. She was just accident prone. Now she looked furtive and guilty. Her eyes were shiny and elusive. It was the look of a dog who has peed on the carpet and is hoping to get away with it.

'What?!' demanded Jess. It's important to seize the initiative at such times.

'You're back early.' Her mum frowned. 'Everything all right?'

'The party sucked,' said Jess, 'and these shoes are killing me. I want a bath.' She kicked off her shoes and walked down the hall towards the privacy of her own room and the comfort of her favourite posters and her old teddy bear Rasputin.

Jess's room was the one thing about her home life that was just perfect. It was a ground-floor room at the back, overlooking their garden. It was private. Nobody could see in. It was quite big. And she had been allowed to paint it purple.

But now her mum sort of barred her way with an uneasy shuffling movement. Jess scowled.

'What?' she demanded again. Her mum was a pacifist when it came to international relations, but she could still put up a good fight at home.

'Great news!' smiled her mum, but the smile wavered and cracked a little. What sort of great news? Jess's weird and rather horrid imagination kicked in. *Great news – a runaway skunk has pooed in your underwear drawer.*

'Granny's coming to live with us,' said her mum. She said it extra fast, so that it sounded like 'Grannyscomingtolivewithus'. As if by getting it out into the open quickly, she would somehow avoid big trouble.

Jess considered the proposal. She loved her granny. OK, so Granny was slightly obsessed with death and sometimes acted a bit old ladyish. She could be boring when she droned on about the past, especially her favourite subject: 'Grisly Operations Suffered by Various Old Codgers of My Acquaintance'. Oh, and there was that other obsession: 'Ghastly Accidents and Fatal Fires Which Scarred My Tragic Childhood'. But at least if Granny came to live with them, it would mean they wouldn't have to go and stay with her in her grim old house that smelt of haddock.

'Cool,' said Jess. 'Now can I get into my room, please, Mum?'

Her mum still barred her way. 'The thing is, darling . . .' Oh no! This was serious. Mum never called her 'darling' unless somebody had died, or another war had broken out. 'I'm really sorry, Jess, but she's going to have to have your room.'

'My room!?' exploded Jess. 'There's a perfectly good spare room upstairs!'

'Yes, but, you see, darling . . . Granny can't manage stairs quite so easily any more. Since Grandpa died and she had that fall, you know – well, her house is too much for her to manage on her own.' Jess was numb with agony. Her lovely room! And she had got it just how she wanted it! It was perfect! 'Granny has to be on the ground floor, love. She can use the ground-floor loo, and we'll convert the old coal shed at the back into a bathroom.'

Jess was too furious to speak. No, wait, she wasn't.

'Where am I supposed to sleep, then?' she snapped. 'Out on the pavement?'

'Don't be silly, love. The spare bedroom upstairs.' Jess's mum had the best bedroom upstairs, the big one at the front. The second-best bedroom was her mum's study. It was lined with bookshelves and there were three filing cabinets and a huge desk. It was just over-flowing with political stuff. From this nerve-centre the local anti-war campaign was organised. Papers lay about everywhere. There were huge piles of antiwar leaflets. Thousands of them. And there were the banners which Jess's mum carried in the marches. The third bedroom was tiny. A box room. Just about enough room for a bed. Barely big enough to accommodate a pet gerbil. Hardly enough room to lie down without having your legs sticking out of the window or your head out on the landing.

'Why can't I have your study?' Jess cried.

'Jess, darling, you know why not. I need that study. There's so much stuff. You know I have to keep the peace campaign going, love. It's for your generation – to give you a future. To stop war.'

'Well, I love war!' Jess's temper snapped. A wave of red-hot fury washed through her. 'I think war's terrific!

And when I leave school I'm going to join the army and kill as many people as possible! Now please can I get into my room for what may possibly be the last time!' She pushed past her mother.

What on earth . . . What had happened to her room? All her clothes had been pulled out of the drawers and tossed into cardboard boxes. The posters had been taken down and rolled up. It wasn't her room any longer. Evicted already.

'It looks like a bomb's hit it!' cried Jess. Usually it was her mum who bawled out those very words about her room. This was a moment of revenge. But it wasn't much comfort.

'If you'd ever seen a room that had *really* been hit by a bomb, you wouldn't use that phrase so lightly!' yelled her mum, trying to make Jess feel guilty in a really horrid way. 'I've just started packing up your stuff, because the thing is, Granny's coming tomorrow. It's very short notice. Her neighbour rang me this evening. Apparently she's strained some ligaments in her knee and it'll be much easier to look after her here.'

'OK, OK, I get the picture!' Jess bent down and scooped some clothes into a bag: her jeans, a T-shirt and sweatshirt, nice warm socks and trainers.

'Oh, there's a good girl!' gushed her mother. 'You

are a darling, Jess. With the two of us working on it, we'll soon have it sorted.'

'I'm not working on it!' screamed Jess. 'As I'm obviously in the way, I'm going! Take my room! I won't be around to inconvenience you any more!' And she strode to the front door, went out and slammed it, hard. She ran off down the street – barefoot, of course, apart from her fishnet tights – and didn't stop until she could put on her socks and trainers in the shadow of the bus shelter. Of course, she had to put them on over the tights. Style-wise, she was now a disaster from the knees down – until she could find somewhere to change into her jeans. Also her bra was still damp. She was dying to rip it off. But she couldn't do it here, in the street. It was like a horrible dream. She had to find somewhere.

Her feet were blistered from walking home in the terrible party shoes. Still, the socks helped. Jess limped off up the road. At the far end of the street was a main road with shops and some public toilets. She'd go and change into her jeans and stuff there. Maybe she could even live there. Where was she going to spend the rest of the night? Should she go to Flora's and wait for her to come home from the party? If only Flora's mum and dad would adopt her. If only a kindly and amazingly wealthy old gentleman could find her and take her home, like in a Victorian novel.

No, wait, that sounded a bit sinister. Maybe a kind and amazingly wealthy old lady instead. A kind old lady film director. A kind old lady film director from Hollywood. Who would say, *'I can make you big in movies. We can get you a new set of boobs, no problem. Choose a pair from this catalogue. I have a house by the ocean and you'll have your own suite there, with a balcony where you can breakfast on freshly-squeezed Californian orange juice and toasted muffins, while turquoise birds sing sweetly in the lemon groves nearby. And as I have no children, Jess, I am going to make you my heir.'*

Jess reached the Ladies loo. It was locked.

Chapter 6

What now? She couldn't ring Flora. She didn't want to be reminded of the worst party ever. She didn't want to hear all the jokes about her boobs and her new role as a soup kitchen. Perhaps this was the moment to emigrate to Australia or begin a distinguished career as a street urchin and pickpocket. On the other hand, it was horribly cold and she was hungry – and she needed the loo. Not for the first time, Jess wished she were a dog. Preferably Ben Jones's.

Suddenly she realised where to go: Fred's. He only lived round the corner and he had said he planned to spend the evening lying on the sofa watching something horribly violent on TV. As yet he would not have heard of her humiliation. And he had a bathroom. Jess ran to Fred's house and rang the bell. Fred appeared, tousled and crumpled from hours of violent films. He did seem pleased to see her, however.

'My parents are out drinking themselves into an early grave,' he explained. He invited her in and told her to help herself to coffee.

'In a minute,' said Jess. 'Just let me get changed in your bathroom, first. And please – can I have a shower?'

'Sure,' said Fred. 'Of course, I never perform hygienic acts myself, being a lovable scamp of repulsive personal habits. But I have observed a shower in the bathroom and I believe it works.'

Never had a house seemed so warm, pleasant, modern and clean. The bathroom was immaculate. Jess had a wonderful, long, streamy hot shower. Every last scrap of minestrone was sluiced off her shining bod and went swirling away into oblivion. The soupy smell was replaced by the zing of Fred's mum's mint and tea tree shower gel. Then Jess washed her hair with some marigold and nettle shampoo and conditioned it with honeysuckle and wild rose. It was the nearest she was ever going to get to gardening.

After drying herself, Jess tried all Fred's mum's moisturisers and body lotions. There was something secretly delicious about snooping in somebody else's bathroom cabinets. Jess found some pills called 'Pariet' which had been prescribed for Fred's dad. His name was written on the box: Mr Peter Parsons. She wondered what the pills were for, but unfortunately the label didn't reveal any indiscreet details.

It must be a bit odd having a man living in the house. She hadn't actually gone to stay with her dad since he had moved to St Ives several years ago. He often came up to town to see friends, and that was when she saw him. Jess felt sad for a moment at the thought of her dad's lonely pills in his lonely bathroom cabinet. 'Mr Tim Jordan, three tablets, once a day in the morning.' What if he dropped dead in his studio? Would he ever be found? A tear trickled down Jess's nose. Curse this premenstrual tension! By tomorrow it would be worse. By tomorrow she would be weeping over nursery rhymes and ads for wholesome brown bread.

She got dressed, put on her warm clothes – minus a bra, of course, because she hadn't managed to grab a spare – and went down to the sitting room. The film was still on.

'Sorry about this,' said Fred. 'Only five minutes more. I just want to see this bloody massacre again. There's a great decapitation sequence in the supermarket.'

'Why are boys interested in all this bloodthirsty, macho stuff?' said Jess. 'If you were a decent human being you would be offering me a delightful snack, instead of wallowing in horrors which you admit yourself you have already memorised.'

Immediately Fred stabbed the remote and the TV went off. It was suddenly very quiet.

'So, how was the party?' he asked.

Jess sighed. 'The party sucked. I suffered total humiliation of the sort which I can't bear to describe. Then I limped home in shoes designed by a woman-hating sadist, only to discover that my mum had evicted me from my room because my granny has to come and live with us from, like, tomorrow. So I'm homeless.'

'You think you've got problems?' said Fred. 'Earlier this evening my parents enacted a suicide pact in the garden shed with a range of pesticides. They left a note saying that I am not their true son, but was foisted on them by Satan during a visit to Weymouth. Shortly after 6.30 my left leg got gangrene and fell off, and my ears started pumping out bacteria which will destroy the world. Worst of all, the pizza's past its sell-by date.'

Jess began to feel a bit better. She examined Fred's kitchen and discovered he was lying about the pizza. It was perfectly, divinely fresh and scattered lightly with just the sort of pepperoni she adored.

'Sorry,' he admitted. 'It was just an excuse. I was too

lazy to put it in the oven so I just pigged out on peanut butter sandwiches.'

'Useless, idle, exploitative, male chauvinist drone!' she scolded him – she had picked up some useful insults from her mum over the years. Also, whenever she was with Fred, she started to talk like him, in elaborate old-fashioned sneers. 'This is how you switch an oven on – though I don't expect you to grasp it immediately.'

Jess twirled the cooker's dial and within twenty minutes they were tucking into a sizzling pizza, washed down with freshly-squeezed orange juice. After their meal they lay down on a sofa each in the sitting room and watched music videos.

Eventually Fred's parents came home. They didn't look at all drunk. Jess was relieved. Fred's dad came into the room first.

'Hello,' he intoned in his strange dull vicar-like voice. 'What's the score?'

'I'm sorry!' said Jess, scrambling up and putting on her most innocent and plaintive expression. 'I had a bit of a row with my mum and I've taken refuge under your roof – I'm really sorry for intruding.'

Fred's dad gave her a slow, puzzled look. 'No,' he said, ploddingly, 'I meant, what's the score?'

'It's the football,' Fred explained to Jess, and tossed the remote over to his dad. Within seconds a smear of football-noise blotted out all possibility of conversation. Jess escaped to the kitchen, where she could hear Fred's mum clattering about.

Jess apologised for having had the pizza, apologised for creating a mess and thanked Fred's mum for her hospitality. Jess had been brought up by a woman who believed in politeness more passionately than anyone has ever believed in God. *Help*, Jess was thinking, as she apologised to Fred's mum, *I hope I put all her cosmetics and lotions and stuff back in exactly the right places.*

Fred's mum was always friendly and nice. She had fluffy hair and looked like a teddy bear. 'You're very welcome, Jess – thanks for keeping Fred company,' she beamed. 'Do you want to stay the night? You can have Fred's room – he can sleep on the sofa.'

'Oh, could I?' cried Jess gratefully. 'Only I've had this mega-row with my mum, and I don't think I can face her again tonight.'

'OK, but we must ring her if she doesn't know where you are,' said Fred's mum. 'Don't worry, Jess! I'll talk to her.'

Within seconds the deal was done. Jess's mum was reassured without Jess having to speak to her, squirm and apologise or anything. She thanked Fred's mum effusively. She really was the best teddy bear in the world, apart from Rasputin.

'You're so kind!' gushed Jess.

'Oh no, Jess, it's a pleasure to have you. Any time. And your mum is such a wonderful person.'

Jess gawped. Her mum, a wonderful person? Had Fred's mum got her wires crossed and was she, in fact, thinking of Flora's mum instead?

'She's an inspiration to us all,' Fred's mum went on, making Jess a hot chocolate without even thinking to offer it first – the act of a saint. 'She's always so vibrant and positive, and she really cares about trying to make the world a better place. And she's got such a fine bone structure.'

This was an amazing speech. It was certainly news to Jess that her mother was some kind of community idol and, furthermore, physically attractive in a skeletal kind of way, but she decided just to enjoy the feeling instead of arguing. Secretly, of course, she knew that her mum was a rancid, rat-haired old bat, but PR was an impor- tant skill in today's modern world, and it would do no good for the awful truth to get out. As the daughter of a vibrant, positive and attractive political activist, she was apparently welcome here. So why argue?

An hour later, Jess was installed in Fred's bed. Fred's mother had insisted on supplying clean sheets and a fresh pair of Fred's pyjamas to sleep in.

'I'd lend you a pair of mine,' she confided, 'but I'm afraid I sleep in my birthday suit.' Jess tried not to scream aloud. The thought of Fred's parents involved in nude sleeping was too awful to endure. Jess just hoped their nocturnal nakedness wouldn't be audible.

Fred seemed delighted at the opportunity of spending the night on the sofa in a sleeping bag. There were especially violent movies on during the early hours, apparently: movies too gory for the under-18s, too gory for the under-40s; movies which had a 'Blindfolds and Earplugs Only' certificate.

Jess found it hard to go to sleep. She couldn't bear to think what it would have been like on the floor of the Ladies loo, if it'd been open. There was something strangely distracting about sleeping in Fred's bed. And there was also a perverse kind of thrill involved in wearing Fred's pyjamas, even though she had never consciously fancied him.

Goodness knows what it would have been like if she had been offered similar accommodation by Ben Jones's mother. If she ever had the opportunity to wear Ben Jones's pyjamas, she would never wash again.

She would never take them off. She would wear them for the rest of her life, even when she was an old lady. But no! She must not think about Ben Jones. He had witnessed her humiliation and from now on he would regard her as nothing more than a complete and utter idiot. And so would everyone else.

Chapter 7

Jess was walking down a street, a crowded street, maybe Oxford Street, and all the faces coming towards her were staring, staring. Suddenly she realised she was only wearing a bra from the waist up. No T-shirt. No top. People were leering and jeering. Desperate, awful shame flooded over her. Suddenly, at her feet, a manhole cover opened, in the middle of the pavement, and Fred looked out. He held up his hand.

'Come on – quick!' he grinned, and Jess jumped in beside him. The cover slammed shut over their heads. Fred didn't let go of her. They were running hand in hand across a vast beach where an ocean growled and crashed. Shining birds wheeled and plummeted overhead and rainbows danced in the spray. 'We're going to see the Tiger!!' cried Fred. Jess didn't know what he meant, but she held on tight. His hand was warm.

Suddenly, she awoke. For a split second she could still feel the grasp of Fred's hand, then it vanished. She was in Fred's bedroom. A huge poster depicting intergalactic warfare gloomed down at her. Welcome back to the real world of testosterone. It was eight o'clock. At home, of course, Jess would have turned over and gone on sleeping for another four hours: her Sunday treat. But she could hear somebody moving about downstairs, so she got up and quickly dressed.

Fred's mum was making tea. 'Tea, Jess? A waffle?'

'A waffle! Wow, yes, please! I could live here for ever! Are you looking for a lodger?'

Fred's mum laughed. 'We'll have it in here. Fred's fast asleep on the sofa.' She closed the kitchen door. 'His mouth is wide open, as if he's singing. Have you ever seen Fred asleep?'

'Oh, frequently!' laughed Jess. 'Don't forget we're in the same set for French, English and history!'

It was warm and merry in the kitchen. A cat dozed on the laundry basket by the French windows. Sunlight twinkled in the garden beyond.

'I love this time of year!' said Fred's mum as she expertly manoeuvred a waffle on to a plate and handed Jess the maple syrup. 'Summer – flowers everywhere, it gets light so early. And not long till the summer holidays, eh?'

Jess agreed. Adults often raved madly about the summer, flowers, etc. Jess's mum even went into rhapsodies about her bean plants. And when it was time to dig up the first new potatoes, she would come indoors with her hands covered in mud and a grin of pure ecstasy on her face. Perhaps it was because there wasn't a man in her life.

Jess wondered what it would be like to have a stepfather. She had often fantasised about recruiting a rich one. But she supposed no rich man would look twice at her mum. She was the sort of woman admired mainly by other women. She didn't even pluck her eyebrows. They looked like a hedge in a gale.

Anyway, Jess wouldn't want a frightening controlfreak like Flora's dad in her life. Fred's dad seemed OK. Big, dull, cuddly, addicted to football. What more could one expect of a male person? It must be intensely boring being a man. The very sound of a football crowd made Jess feel depressed, like hymn singing on Sundays. But all men seemed to have to be addicted to sport. Although, come to think of it, Jess's own dad was completely uninterested in sports of all kinds.

Jess hadn't seen him for quite a while. But he'd be

coming up to town in the summer holidays. He was the very opposite of Fred's dad. He was thin, anxious-looking, nervy and not at all cuddly. On the rare occasions when Jess saw her father, he gave her a hug carefully, as if he had prepared for it by reading a manual called *How to Cuddle Your Child* and he was afraid he would get it wrong. Bless him, the moron!

The waffle was delicious, and Fred's mother, angel that she was, tried to tempt Jess to a second.

'No, no, thanks, I really mustn't,' said Jess. 'I ought to get off home because we've got to get ready for Granny coming. I've got to move out of my room.'

'That's hard,' sympathised Fred's mum. 'But think of the Brownie points you'll accumulate. Your mum will feel so guilty about it, she'll never dare say no to you again!'

Jess hadn't considered this possibility. It was certainly a cheerful thought. She thanked Fred's mum effusively and they tiptoed towards the front door. They paused by the open door to the sitting room and looked in for a moment. Fred was lying fast asleep, half out of his sleeping bag, but his mouth wasn't open any more. In fact, he was sucking his thumb. *Oh my goodness*, thought Jess, *how unbelievably sweet!*

'For heaven's sake don't tell anybody!' whispered his mum. 'He'd never live it down!'

Jess walked home in five minutes, but she could feel her warm, positive mood slipping away with every step, and a chilly foreboding creeping back over her. She wondered in agony how she was ever going to get all her stuff into that tiny box room. Her huge posters would just have to stay rolled up under the bed. And what about her clothes? There wasn't even a wardrobe, just a tiny chest of drawers about big enough to hold a Barbie doll outfit.

And, oh no! Her Barbie dolls! All twenty-eight of them! She hadn't played with them for years, of course – not for years and years and years. And years. They lived in a huge cardboard box under her bed. She was saving them up for when she had a little girl. (By genetic engineering, obviously, or cloning. No man would ever want to marry her.) But even though she never ever played with her Barbies now, she would always keep them. They were part of her history.

The box room. No bigger than a coffin. It would be like being buried. Maybe she wouldn't keep her Barbies after all. She would make a huge bonfire in the back garden. She would burn her clothes. She would burn all her old toys (except her old teddy bear Rasputin, obviously – he was more of a guru and personal trainer than a toy). She would burn all her make-up. She would shave off all her hair and burn that. She would wear only a pair of Oriental black pyjamas. She would sleep in the box room on a small mat made of rushes. The only item in the room would be a plain white saucer for her tears. *Then* they'd be sorry.

By the time she got home, her insides had screwed themselves up into a dreadful knot, and she wished she hadn't had the waffle. Indeed, there was a danger that any moment the waffle might, in some rather grisly sense, be born again. She was dreading seeing her mum. Would she be angry? How angry? Or perhaps she had gone stark staring mad and would be crouching in a corner mumbling, her clothes reduced to rags, muesli scattered on her head?

But her mum's car was missing. Oh no! Had she gone to drive off a cliff somewhere, leaving a note? *Owing to the difficulties with my daughter I no longer wish to be a burden to her.*

Jess let herself in and immediately saw that her mum had indeed left a note, on the hall table.

Dear Jess,

I've gone to get Granny, as it's quite a long drive and I want to be back by teatime. Sorry about yesterday. It's really unfair of me expecting you to move into that poky little box room, so I've moved into it myself. All my stuff is in there in plastic bin bags. You can have my bedroom. I've put all your stuff in there and you can do whatever you like with it.

Love Mum

Jess ran upstairs and charged into what had been her mum's bedroom – the best room upstairs, by miles. It had two windows! It had a built-in wardrobe! It even had a little fireplace where Jess was already planning to have a real log fire! Tears of joy ran down Jess's cheeks. Curse this premenstrual tension. But her mum was so kind! Jess loved her so much! Here was this lovely, palatial room and she could do whatever she liked with it. Her mum had placed Rasputin the bear on the bed and he seemed to be waving to her – regally, of course. This was the best Sunday since Sundays were invented.

The phone rang. A cold spear of fear went through Jess's heart. She was sure her mother had been killed in a road accident. Just at the very moment when she loved her more than everyone else in the world put together, she had been cruelly snatched away. Jess fell on the phone.

'Yes?' she gasped, preparing for the cold voice of a police officer or possibly an Accident and Emergency nurse.

'Hey, Jess!' It was Flora. 'Everybody's dying to hear – what exactly happened last night between you and Whizzer?'

Chapter 8

Jess and Flora met in a cafe. Unfortunately, their part of town was completely lacking in style, and the only place open on Sundays was a little religious charity place which sold snacks made by poor people in Africa.

'Is this actually food or some kind of building material?' Jess growled as she tried to free her teeth from a cereal bar made of tree bark, gravel and superglue.

'It's OK, we should eat more of this sort of stuff,' Flora assured her. 'The starving –'

'Yes, yes, I know! Don't give me a hard time about the starving! I get enough political harassment from Mum at home! There's no need to start preaching just because it's Sunday!'

'Sssssh!' whispered Flora.

The middle-aged woman who ran the place

looked disapprovingly at them over her owly glasses. She was polishing some mugs adorned with portraits of Jesus.

'Please don't say anything loud and satanic,' Flora whispered. 'Or we'll get thrown out, and there's nowhere else open.'

'So how was the party?' asked Jess. 'How did you get on with Mackenzie? I hope you broke his heart with a resounding crack audible at the North Pole?'

'He is so cool!' confided Flora. 'We spent the whole evening together. He's really witty and, like, confident and stuff, and he told me I'm beautiful, which is rubbish, of course.' Flora's modesty could be irritating. She was always insisting that she hated her eyes, nose, mouth, skin, hair, etc, despite the fact that when He created Flora, God was on tip-top form and really cooking on gas.

On that day He also made the flamingos, the dolphins, the rainbows and a divine apple crumble with custard. By the time He got around to creating Jess, however, He had rather run out of steam and had a slight headache, and could only manage a couple of other things – toads, baboons and possibly methane – before needing to take an aspirin and have a lie-down.

'But what about you?' asked Flora. 'What happened with Whizzer? Did you puke all over him or did he puke all over you?' Jess was amazed for a moment. The soup! This must be something to do with the minestrone. 'He said you'd been sick all over him and you ran off to the loo and then you went home. You poor thing! If you'd told me I would have looked after you and everything! What was it? Food poisoning?'

Jess was speechless for a moment. Saved by a rumour of vomit! Maybe the strange tale of her bags of soup wasn't widely known after all. Jess was tempted to tell the whole story to Flora. Normally she told her absolutely everything. But this time . . . maybe not. It was a chance of a great escape, and Jess seized it.

'Yeah,' she said eventually. 'Must have been something I ate.' Wanting desperately to change the subject from vomit, though, Jess went on, 'So what about Ben? I sort of bumped into him just as I was leaving. Not in a stylish way, either. More like a kind of bison colliding with a barn door. Who did he get off with? I suppose he was mobbed by lovelorn maidens all wanting a piece of him?'

'No,' said Flora. 'He was talking to me and Mackenzie quite a lot. They're thinking of starting a band and . . . well, they asked me to be lead singer in it.' Flora looked ever so slightly furtive as she completed this speech, and sort of flinched very prettily, like a shepherdess who has trodden in some sheep's poo.

Jess's heart leapt right out of her mouth, completed two circuits of the cafe and re-entered her body at speed through her right nostril. It was amazing nobody noticed. Ben Jones had asked Flora to be in his band! Of course, she had to smile and look thrilled to bits for Flora, though the sky went dark, and the coffee in her cup turned into the urine of a vampire bat.

'He asked you to be in his band?' Jess blurted out. 'That's fantastic! You'll be on TV by Christmas! I shall wait at the stage door and cry out feebly for your autograph as you sweep out to your waiting limousine, but my words will be lost in the howl of the crowd . . . You will be blinded by the flashing cameras of the paparazzi . . .'

'Don't be silly,' said Flora. 'I don't suppose it'll come to anything. I can't sing anyway. We've got nowhere to practise. And I don't suppose my parents will let me. My mum's got a thing about protecting me from loud noises because I had so many ear infections when I was little.'

'No, no – you're gonna be big!' Suddenly Jess couldn't eat another mouthful of the cereal bar, not even for the sake of the starving. 'You're gonna be massive – global! Intergalactic! People will be watching your videos on Mars!' Jess managed, with a heroic effort, to go on smiling.

'You can come to our rehearsals,' said Flora, looking guilty.

'I'm not sure about that.' Jess frowned. No way would she hang around at their rehearsals, like some kind of sad groupie. 'I'm going to be really busy getting my new room ready. I'm going to paint it purple and fling leopardskin throws about. What I thought was going to be a disaster has turned into a great interior design opportunity. Thanks, bizarrely, to my granny.'

'My granny's just gone off for a holiday in Barbados!' said Flora. 'She'll probably be water-skiing by now. Or snorkelling or something.'

'Why does your granny have to be so glamorous?' enquired Jess acidly. 'Doesn't she know grannies are supposed to hobble off to bingo and moan about their arthritis? Barbados! Honestly! What a showoff!'

'Your granny is heaps nicer than mine,' said Flora guiltily. 'She's so funny. I hope her knee gets better soon. And I'm dying to see your new room. Can I help you to paint it?' Flora was trying so horribly hard to be nice. She would win an Olympic gold medal for niceness. Jess felt completely paralysed by it. It was like being trapped in icing sugar and nibbled to death by pink teddy bears.

Jess stood up. 'I've gotta go,' she said. 'I've got heaps to do on my room.'

Flora had to go, too. She had already done her homework, of course – and possibly ironed it and sprinkled it with rosewater. She was planning to spend the evening chatting online with Mackenzie about the band.

On the way home Jess dropped in at the petrol station and spent the last of her pocket money on a bunch of flowers for Granny. She felt, on the whole, she would rather not have a granny who went water-skiing in Barbados. It was going a bit too far. For Jess's granny, luxurious fun consisted of trying out a new flavour of cough lozenge. Cherry instead of honey and lemon was her idea of living dangerously.

Jess arranged the flowers in Granny's room. It didn't look like her room any more, and now she had the best bedroom upstairs, she didn't mind about giving up the downstairs one. Jess went upstairs and stuck all her posters on the wall. She adored her new room. She made plans to cover the floor with astroturf and paint the ceiling sky blue with aeroplanes. Or perhaps she would adorn the walls with red velvet and make herself a four-poster bed with an antique Venetian shawl thrown carelessly across it and old brown leather-bound books on the bedside table. And a candle in an iron candlestick. And a stuffed owl in a niche. Looking a bit like Fred with his hood up.

It was five o'clock. Where were Mum and Granny? Should she start to worry? Jess decided instead to make herself a cheese sandwich. She hadn't eaten anything since the gravel and glue cereal bar at the Christian cafe. She hoped the catering in heaven was a bit more appetising. She had just taken a huge mouthful of sandwich when the phone rang.

'Jess, love, I'm so sorry, we're halfway home and the clutch has burned out,' said her mum. 'We're going to stay the night in a B&B. Can you cope?'

'Of course I can!' cried Jess indignantly, even though the shadow of a werewolf was already visible on the opposite wall.

'Well, maybe you'd like to have Flora over, or something – to keep you company,' suggested her mum.

This seemed like an excellent idea. If Flora came over, Jess could snoop on her Facebook chat with

Mackenzie, and perhaps even learn a thing or two about Ben Jones's secrets. Maybe, who knows, Ben Jones himself might appear – virtually, that is. His profile name was apparently Six Toes. Jess wondered if he really did have six toes. Would she ever get to see his feet? She was sure they would be fragrant and sacred, not smelly like other boys' feet.

Jess rang Flora. 'Guess what! I'm Home Alone. Wanna come over?'

'Oh, wow, yes!' said Flora. 'And shall I see if I can bring Mackenzie and Ben Jones?'

'What, seriously?' A thrill ran down Jess's spine. 'Wow! Bring it on!' she cried. 'Yes per-leease! But the place is a complete tip!'

'Great!' answered Flora. 'If it's a complete tip already then there's no danger of us making a mess, is there?'

Jess rang off and looked around in a panic. She was supposed to be doing her homework. But in less than an hour Ben Jones might be sitting right there on her sofa! His divine bum would leave an imprint so sacred, nobody would ever be allowed to sit there again. But could she transform herself into a thing of beauty in less than an hour? Could she design herself a pair of eyebrows that would break his heart for ever? She could but try. She seized her tweezers and uttered a faint prayer for supernatural help. After all, she had eaten most of a religious cereal bar at lunchtime. She hoped such heroism had not gone unnoticed by those above.

Chapter 9

Amazing! Unbelievable! Mackenzie and Ben Jones were sitting on her sofa! Really sitting there, in flesh and blood! Mackenzie was cute, with dark curls and a dangerous smile. Ben Jones was blond, silent and charismatic. This was so the most exciting moment of Jess's life so far.

'Wanna Pepsi?' she asked.

'Got anything else?' asked Mackenzie. 'Pepsi makes him fart.' He nodded towards Ben. Ben groaned and thumped him. This was certainly a romantic start to the evening.

'Haven't you got a beer or something, Jess?' asked Flora, looking quite annoyed at Jess's painful lack of style.

'No. Sorry. My mum doesn't drink, and we never get wine or beer in unless we have visitors we're trying to impress,' confessed Jess. 'We haven't had any vodka in the house since the prime minister dropped by.'

There was a silence. The boys looked blank. Ben waggled his feet and stared at them. Jess was terrified. It was going to be a disaster.

'My parents have got a wine cellar,' said Flora.

'Wow! Ace! Wicked! Let's go there, then,' said Mackenzie.

'We can't!' yelled Flora in panic. 'My parents are at home.'

The boys looked disappointed.

'I can't offer you the crystal chandeliers and champagne of Flora's place,' remarked Jess, 'but that kind of stuff is so Last Century. Nowadays everybody's into dry toast and tap water. It's kind of, you know, Buddhist.' Ben looked puzzled. Mackenzie looked bored. It had been a mistake to mention Buddhism.

'Remember last Christmas?' said Mackenzie. 'We went round Carter's and raided his dad's bar? Man, did he booze! He sploffed his fozza with a Red Stinker.'

Jess sighed. Boys had a language of their own. They could be talking about drink. But it could equally be a reference to sport, or a video game. Or even war. This evening was beginning to be a bit of a disappointment, conversation-wise. Ben was apparently incapable of joined-up speech. And Mackenzie was talking in Hungarian.

Jess began to rewrite the dialogue in her head, à la Jane Austen.

'Good afternoon, Miss Jordan, Miss Barclay,' said Sir Benjamin Jones, with a distinguished bow. 'May we expect the pleasure of your company at the ball at Netherbourne next month?'

'So what have you got to drink, Jess? Apart from Pepsi?' demanded Flora rather irritably.

'I think I may have some chocolate milkshake,' said Jess, secretly aware that it was probably past its sell-by date.

'Yeah! Ace! Milkshake! Wicked!' shouted Mackenzie. 'Gimme milkshake – straight into the vein!'

Jess couldn't help noticing that he hadn't said *please*.

'What about you, Ben?' she said. She was trying to make her voice sound low and sultry, but unfortunately, as she spoke, a little drop of spit shot out of her mouth and landed on Ben's shirt. He flinched. Oh no! That was the end of everything! She had hoped to seduce him and had instead spat on his clothing.

Ben Jones said, 'Er – I'm OK, thanks.' He didn't brush the spit off or anything, although Jess knew that he knew it was there. She could see it still glistening. Luckily Flora and Mackenzie were gazing into each other's eyes and hadn't noticed.

'I'd like some milkshake, too, please, Jess,' said Flora. 'I just *so* adore chocolate.' She licked her lips and sighed. Both the boys gawped at her, clearly wishing they could be turned into Easter eggs right there and then.

Jess went out to the kitchen. The milkshake was only one day past its sell-by date. Jess sniffed it. It didn't smell too bad, although there was a faint whiff of garlic about it from one of her mum's jars of salad dressing which had been standing next to it in the fridge, with the lid off. So far, so good: a chocolate'n'garlic milkshake only just beginning to go off. But there was only enough left to fill one glass.

Wait! If she used smaller glasses, maybe she could fill two. She found a couple of wine glasses and poured the milkshake into them. Then she got a Pepsi for herself. Then she ate a cracker to dry her spit up, so she wouldn't shower Ben Jones with saliva again. She inhaled a cracker crumb, choked and had a coughing fit. Her eyes watered. Her mascara ran. She reapplied it in the downstairs cloakroom: hurry, hurry, hurry! She smudged it. Would she manage to get back into the living room before one of her guests died of old age?

Jess re-entered the sitting room red-faced from coughing, and with her left eye so smudged, she looked like some kind of pirate. It became clear the moment she entered that it wouldn't have mattered if she had grown a third eye out in the kitchen and lined it with red mascara – nobody would have noticed.

Flora had moved and was sprawling on the rug at the feet of the boys. It would be impossible for anybody sitting on the sofa to avoid looking down her cleavage and up her skirt at the same time. Jess peeped sideways at Ben Jones to see if he was looking down Flora's cleavage. He certainly was. Well, he'd have had to fix his eyes on the ceiling to avoid it.

'Cheers,' said Mackenzie, picking up the glass of milkshake. He downed it in a single gulp.

'Haven't you got any bigger glasses, Jess?' asked Flora with a superior little frown. 'These are wine glasses.'

'I know these are wine glasses, for goodness' sake,' snapped Jess. 'The tumblers are dirty. What does it matter anyway?'

'No need to get narky with me,' said Flora with a strange, hostile glare. She turned to the boys, and Jess saw her face glide from irritation to seduction. Mackenzie and Ben were both looking down Flora's cleavage with the kind of eager, addictive stare that suggested a crucial football match might be taking place across her chest.

'Tell me about this band of yours,' said Jess.

'Yeah, it's ace! Wicked!' said Mackenzie. 'We're gonna start band practice as soon as we can find somewhere to rehearse – hey! What about here?'

'You can't,' said Jess hastily. 'My granny's going to be living with us.'

'A granny!' said Mackenzie. 'Cool! Is she hot? Maybe she could front our band!' Everybody laughed, although Jess felt slightly sick and guilty, and wished her granny lived in Alaska and had never been mentioned.

'We can't rehearse in my house,' said Flora, 'because of my dad. I won't even be able to tell my parents I'm going to sing in the band. Jess – when I go to band practice, can I say I'm coming round to see you?'

'Yeah,' said Jess. 'Whatever.'

A dull ache sprang up in her insides. She dreaded a phone conversation with Flora's terrifying father. 'Where is Flora exactly, Jess, please?' he would say, in his ferocious successful-businessman's sort of snarly voice. Jess almost fainted at the thought. This evening was getting worse and worse. It was turning into an absolute nightmare. Ben Jones had hardly spoken a single word, yet. There was only one thing for it – to take refuge in fantasy.

'It is quite close indoors,' said Sir Benjamin. 'Would you care to take a turn around the shrubbery, Miss Jordan?'

'I should like that very well, Sir Benjamin,' said Jess, putting down her Pepsi – no, no, her teacup – with a trembling hand.

'The azaleas are in bloom. It is a lovely sight. Miss Flora, would you be so kind as to clear the tea things and attend to the fire?'

Miss Flora nodded modestly and obediently. Such a sweet girl. A shame about her massive red nose and irregular green teeth.

'So, what are we going to call ourselves?' asked Mackenzie. 'How about Wicked? That would be wicked. Ha ha!'

Jess supposed this was what Flora referred to as Mackenzie's rapier wit. 'Haven't you thought of the name yet?' she asked. 'I would have thought of the name first. That's the best bit, thinking of the name. After that it's downhill all the way.'

'We're still fighting about it,' said Flora. There was

something irritating about that *we*. So they were a *we*, were they? The three of them. Having fun fighting excitingly.

'So what's the shortlist?' demanded Jess.

'Well, Mackenzie thinks it should be Insane Carrot,' Flora began, 'B.J. likes Killer Toads and I go for Archaeology.'

Jess tried to look interested. But instead she was mesmerised by Flora casually calling Ben 'B.J.' She had never heard him called that by anybody else. It must be a special nickname invented for him by Flora.

'How about Poisonous Trash?' suggested Jess between gritted teeth.

The phone rang. Jess suddenly felt a lurch of guilt. OK, her mum had said it was all right for Flora to be there – but what about the boys?

'Quiet!' she hissed and grabbed the phone.

'Jess?'

'Dad!'

'How are you, love? What have you been up to? Sorry I haven't rung for a couple of weeks – I've had a rather tragic bout of flu.'

It's my dad! Jess mouthed. 'S'cuse me, Dad – I'll just go and use the upstairs phone – we've got some people here.' She replaced the phone and pulled a face. 'I'll be right back,' she promised. Oh, why did her dad have to call tonight of all nights? His timing was catastrophic.

She picked up the phone in her mother's study. 'Yeah, Dad, sorry to hear about the flu,' she said. 'Are you better now?'

'Still got a bit of a cough,' he said. 'Wait a minute – there's one coming along now. It sounds like a hen-house being demolished – listen!' He coughed extensively to demonstrate. Such a hypochondriac! Jess loved her dad, but over the years she had learned a lot more than she cared to know about his lungs and his large intestine. Jess asked him how life was in St Ives, and made him promise to let her come and stay.

'Well, I suppose we could arrange something.' He hesitated, as if having your daughter to stay involved building a whole east wing and hiring a camel-train of three hundred to accompany her on her journey. 'Although I'm not sure where you could sleep. Maybe I could get some kind of large kennel . . .'

'I can sleep anywhere, Dad,' Jess assured him. 'On the sofa. On the floor. I don't care. I haven't even seen your new house and you've been there for ages. And it's by the sea. It's such a waste.'

'I'll talk it over with Mummy,' said her dad. 'I'm not

sure she would let you come and stay. She thinks I have no discipline. You'll have to promise to read the Bible all the time and go to bed at 7.30.'

'7.30!' cried Jess in mock outrage. 'I'd be fast asleep *long* before that!'

'And you'd have to vacuum the house from top to bottom before a meek breakfast of tinned fish and vitamin pills,' said her dad.

'Well, obviously,' replied Jess. 'And I'd perform ten-mile walks in sensible shoes.'

'That's settled, then,' said her dad.

But Jess wasn't at all sure that it was. She didn't completely trust her dad not to wriggle out of it. He could go along with swapping jokes for ages and then suddenly – crunch – he'd sort of change gear and go boring and serious and grown-up. And he did just that, right now.

'Could I have a quick word with Mum, please, love? She sent me an e-mail saying she's been having a bit of trouble with Granny.'

Jess hesitated. 'Mum's out,' she admitted. 'She's gone to get Granny and bring her back here to live. But the car broke down on the way home so they're staying the night somewhere.'

'Who's looking after you, then?'

'I don't need anybody to look after me, Dad – I'm perfectly capable of looking after myself!' There was a quiet, anxious pause. She just knew Dad was picking his fingers and beginning to get nervous indigestion.

'But you said you've got friends in?' he asked.

'Yeah, just Flora and a couple of others.'

'Girls, Jess? Or those horrible boy-type things?'

'Mackenzie and Ben Jones from school, Dad – there's no need to sound so disapproving. They're totally harmless. I mean, you were a boy once. You didn't do anything terribly bad, did you?'

'I was an almost ingeniously boring boy,' said her dad, rather sadly. 'The nearest I ever got to a wild night out was organising a disco for my pet hamsters. So what are you doing? Watching some dire film, I suppose?'

'No – the TV isn't even on, Dad. We're just trying to decide on a name for our band.'

'You're in a band? Wow, I'm so out of touch.'

'Well, I'm not actually in it. Flora's the singer. I'm the manager.' Jess liked the idea of being a manager. Perhaps she would offer her services for real. *'I'm the manager of Poisonous Trash.'* It had a certain ring to it.

'And are these boys staying the night? It's half past ten already.'

'Oh, for heaven's sake, Dad, chill out! Of course not. Mackenzie's dad is coming to collect him in five minutes!' Suddenly it didn't seem such a bad deal, having a dad who lived two hundred miles away. It was certainly easier to spin him a line. Reassured by the idea of a grown-up arriving to break up the teenage misbehaviour, Jess's dad rang off, pausing only to enquire whether she had done her homework. Jess assured him she had. Oh well. She could do it tomorrow morning, at the breakfast table.

She raced back downstairs. Mackenzie had joined Flora on the rug – not in any sinister sense. They weren't wrapped around each other. But it sort of signalled he was, well, slightly more *going out with her* than Ben Jones was. Jess found this reassuring. She didn't quite dare to sit down beside Ben on the sofa, though. That would be kind of crude and obvious. So she sat on a low stool beside the TV, although the minute she had arrived there, she began to feel it did nothing for her in the style stakes. One cannot lounge gracefully on a low stool. One can only squat in a Neanderthal manner with one's knees up around one's ears.

'Sorry about that,' she said. 'It was my dad. He lives in St Ives.'

'St Ives?' Ben Jones spoke at last, and looked really impressed. 'Cool! That's . . . by the sea, yeah?'

'Yeah, it's great. I'm going down to stay with him in the holidays,' said Jess. 'You can come if you like. You can all come.'

'Oh, I *so* love the sea!' cried Flora. 'In fact, my granny is at this moment waterskiing in Barbados. That is *so* not fair! I hate her for it!'

'Barbados!?' gasped Ben Jones, and his eyes opened very wide. St Ives was instantly forgotten.

'Barbados!' yelled Mackenzie. 'Wow! Ace! Wicked! Now you're talkin'! And can we all go out and stay with her?'

Compared with Barbados, St Ives was so *boring*. Jess was tempted to seize the nearest heavy object and take a mad swipe at Flora, but managed to control herself. *Rise above it, rise above it*, she thought urgently. *Flora wants to be the centre of attention. So let her be. Let her bask in the limelight. It's a sign of immaturity.* All the same, Jess didn't feel all that mature, crouching in the shadows on her stool.

Suddenly Mackenzie's mobile phone began to tweet. He grabbed it, scowled, stood up and went over to the window.

'What!?' he snapped.

Everybody else eavesdropped silently. Suddenly Jess became aware that Ben Jones was looking at her. Their eyes met, as Flora had predicted. Not across a crowded room, though – across a half-empty one. He performed one of his slow, crooked grins. Just for her.

Something very nice happened in Jess's ribcage, though she wasn't sure what. He had smiled at her – when he could have just stayed ogling Flora's cleavage and imagining himself sunbathing with her in Barbados. Perhaps he did like Jess a little bit after all.

'Why?' grunted Mackenzie on the phone. ' 'S'not fair! . . . All right, all right . . . twenty minutes.' He rang off and turned to face them with a tragic shrug. 'I've gotta go,' he sighed. 'My mum is, like, eating the carpet.'

First, however, he said he needed to visit the bathroom.

'I'll show you where it is!' said Flora, seizing the initiative and giving Jess a meaningful look. Flora and Mackenzie left the room and thundered upstairs. Then there was the murmur of their voices, and a sudden silence.

Ben Jones sniffed – divinely, of course. The silence deepened. Jess began to panic. It was her job to think of something to say, partly because she was the hostess, but also because boys were famously lacking in the ability to form sentences or even have an idea. Except Fred, of course.

'What's your favourite subject?' she blurted out, lamely. This was the most boring thing she had ever said.

Ben Jones looked startled. 'Um . . . physics, I guess,' he replied.

Jess's heart sank. She hated physics. The physics lab stank of rubber and gas. It made her think of hospitals and horrible operations involving iron masks and red-hot tongs.

'Oh yeah! Physics is so cool!' she lied. She had read a magazine once that said you should share your boyfriend's interests. 'What do you want to be when you leave school?' she asked, bizarrely. What was happening to her? She sounded like a careers teacher.

'Er, well, I did think, maybe . . . an investment broker,' said Ben.

Jess frowned. 'What's that?' she asked. 'Sorry to be so dumb.'

Ben Jones laughed, but it wasn't a jeering, sneering sort of laugh; it was a friendly, appreciative one. 'It's to do with, like . . . um, finance,' he said. 'Money. Yeah. What about you?'

Jess panicked. She couldn't tell him – it was too absurd. Oh, all right then.

'I want to be a stand-up comedian!' she confessed.

Ben Jones's eyes widened in amazement and he made a strange little whistling sound.

'Cool!' he commented, eventually. Then he got to his feet and zipped up his jacket.

Silence fell again. Jess clambered up off her stool – with difficulty, as it was so low. Flora would have soared up gracefully like a gazelle disturbed while grazing. Jess lurched up like a hippopotamus struggling out of a swamp.

'Um, how about . . . if you want . . . we can get a . . . er, a coffee tomorrow after school?' said Ben Jones suddenly.

Jess blinked. What? What was that again? Had he just asked her out, or was she imagining things?

'Sorry,' she stammered. 'What did you say?'

Ben Jones blushed. He *blushed*! Wow! This was the best moment of Jess's life so far.

'Yeah, well, um, how about a coffee tomorrow after school?' he repeated.

Jess shrugged and tried to look as if she couldn't quite make up her mind, because there were so many other things she would rather be doing – extra physics, for instance, involving delightful rubber tubes and pieces of charming metal.

'Sure,' she said, with a shy grin. 'Why not?'

Mackenzie and Flora came downstairs and the boys left. Ben Jones did not mention their date the next day in front of the others. He just gave Jess a kind of curt nod. For a moment they shared a secret. It was almost up to the excitement of the Sir Benjamin costume drama in Jess's head. Although Ben did not, alas, drive off down the road in a shining carriage drawn by four fabulous white horses. His only means of transport was a pair of trainers, but they were, Jess had noticed, trainers of a particularly classy sort.

'Guess what!' Jess hissed in ecstasy, as soon as the boys had gone. 'Ben Jones asked me out tomorrow! I have a date! He's asked me out on a date!'

'Terrific!' cried Flora, hugging her and squealing with excitement. 'And guess what! Mackenzie snogged me! In your bathroom! He snogged me and he said I was amazing! If you go out with B.J. and I go out with Mackenzie, it will be so coooooool! Oh, there's just one thing, though. Guess what Mackenzie told me while we were upstairs.'

'What?' demanded Jess impatiently. She didn't want to think about anything else. She just wanted to think about her date with Ben Jones. She wanted to think about it all night long.

'You know Tiffany's brother Jack?'

'Yes, what about him?' What on earth did Flora want to talk about this for?

'Well, do you remember all those flowers and leaves and stuff in the girls' loo at Tiffany's party?'

'Yeah – what?'

'Well, apparently Jack fixed up a camcorder in there, like, hidden in the leaves, and he's got footage of all the girls who went in there. Like CCTV or something! Gross or what! And everyone's going round Tiffany's the day after tomorrow to watch it! Thank goodness I didn't have to go to the loo all evening!'

Flora sighed in relief. Jess couldn't speak. She was absolutely frozen with horror. Flora noticed – eventually. She wasn't a complete monster.

'Oh, no, Jess! You were sick in there, weren't you! You poor thing!'

'It's not that I'm worried about,' said Jess. A paralysing terror was spreading through her entire body, turning every muscle to stone. She didn't have to worry about being sick on CCTV. What she had done was much, much worse. She had stripped to the waist. She had thrown her home-made bra inserts down the loo. And she had washed minestrone off her boobs – while talking to them and calling them Bonnie and Clyde! Jess wondered how far it was to the nearest nunnery, because her life was definitely over.

Chapter 10

'Well . . . Jack says you're the, um, like, star of the CCTV footage.' Ben Jones grinned.

Jess felt sick to death. Here she was, sitting in the Dolphin Cafe with Ben. She had adored him for months. She'd lost track of the number of times she'd written his name on her hand, on her books . . . OK, even the walls of certain public loos. The merest glimpse of him in school had been enough to make her stomach turn somersaults. She had even, once, sat down on a bench he had just been sitting on, and felt the warmth left behind by his bum.

And now he'd actually asked her out! Here they were, on a date – and instead of being thrilled to bits, she was in agony.

'Maybe we could pick up a burger tomorrow, yeah?' he mumbled. 'Like – before?'

'Before what?' stammered Jess.

'Before the *party*, right? At Tiffany's.'

Jess's stomach plummeted through the rather taste-ful Italian floor-tiles of the Dolphin Cafe, through the boiling centre of the earth, and emerged somewhere in the outback where men wear hats with corks dangling from them. Her stomach, it seemed, had emigrated to Australia, and after the shame and humil-iation of the CCTV footage tomorrow night, Jess would have to follow.

'I'm not going!' she blurted out. 'And please, please, promise me you won't go either.'

Ben cocked his eyebrow. 'Hey, chill! It's only, like, a bit of, y'know, *fun*, yeah?'

'Fun?' cried Jess indignantly. 'How would you like it if the girls had fixed up a camera in the boys' loo, and you'd been in there doing private stuff?'

Ben sat quietly for a moment, thinking. Jess tried to bite her nails, but there was really nothing left to bite. She fought off a desperate urge to rip off her shoes and start gnawing at her toenails.

'Don't suppose I'd mind being on CCTV,' Ben shrugged. 'It's just, like, a laugh, right? Whatever it was you – you know, like *did*, it can't be bad. You should just . . . come and have a laugh. That would be well cool. If you don't turn up, people might think you'd, y'know, bottled out.'

Jess knew that the ability to laugh at yourself was a sign of maturity. But she wasn't sure that even a 30-year-old could get through this crisis without screaming aloud and eating their own jeans.

'All the other girls are going,' said Ben. 'Flora's going.'

'It's OK for her,' hissed Jess. 'She didn't even go into the freaking loo. Her bladder must be as big as a bus.'

'She always seems kind of, well, *lucky*,' pondered Ben.

'Too right!' agreed Jess. 'She leads a charmed life. You should see her house. Her dad is this, like, megastar in the bathroom business and her mum looks like a movie star. Their house is amazing. You have to take your shoes off when you go in because the carpets are all cream-coloured. And if their china gets chipped, Flora's mum throws it away. There isn't a single piece of china in my house that isn't chipped.'

Ben stared thoughtfully across the cafe. Jess wondered if perhaps talking about chipped china might not be the ideal way to a boy's heart. But what could she talk about? Movies? Cars? Sport? Music?

She couldn't think of anything for more than a few seconds before her mind went whirling back to the awful subject of CCTV.

'D'you think she really, like, *rates* Mackenzie?' asked Ben suddenly.

Jess forgot about CCTV for a moment. 'Oh yes!' she assured him. 'I think Flora's always had a bit of a thing about him. Plus we've been doing King Charles I in history, and she's majorly mad about him. And I think Mackenzie reminds her of him.'

'What? He reminds her of a *king*?' said Ben, looking puzzled. 'That's weird.'

'Oh no, I mean, that's not why she likes him. That was just my idea. Because Mackenzie's small and dark like Charles I. But there the resemblance ends. Mackenzie does have a head after all.'

'A *head*?' Ben looked even more puzzled.

'You know,' explained Jess. 'Charles I was beheaded. In the Civil War. Roundheads. Cavaliers. Remember?'

Ben nodded. 'Oh yeah,' he said. 'I remember, right. History gets up my nose, so I don't usually listen. But . . . so you reckon Flora's definitely, um, got a thing for Mackenzie? You don't think she's, er . . . going to chuck him, do you? He'd be gutted.'

'Oh no!' Jess assured him. 'Definitely not. She's crazy about him.'

Ben Jones looked carefully at her and nodded slowly. 'Uh-huh. Good.'

Suddenly an awful uneasiness crept into Jess's head. Ben Jones hadn't really wanted to have coffee with her – not for her own sake. Mackenzie had asked him to find out if Flora was serious about him! This wasn't a date. She wasn't being wooed – she was being *grilled*.

Ten minutes ago, Jess had been in agony about the CCTV footage. But at least she had comforted herself with the thought that she was out on a date with Ben Jones. The comfort had seemed rather faint and remote. But at least it had been there. Now, that idea had gone up in smoke.

'I'm sorry,' she said. 'I gotta go. I've got urgent stuff to do at home.' She got up, fast.

Ben Jones looked startled. He scrambled to his feet.

'Wait!' he said. 'So – what about tomorrow? Shall we meet in the burger place – round about 7.30?'

Jess hesitated. 'I'm not sure,' she said. 'I'll have to think about it. I'll text you, OK?'

Ben nodded, and grinned his slanty grin. Her stomach (which seemed to have returned from Australia) performed a cartwheel.

'Go for it,' he said quietly. 'You're a star!'

Jess tossed her head in what she hoped was an elegant and mysterious manner, and walked out. She marched down the street, boiling with emotion. He had said she was a star! Maybe he did want to go out with her after all! By going to the party and facing up to everybody, she could become Ben's *star*. Not exactly his girlfriend, sure, but it was a start. However, Jess doubted if the CCTV footage would show her in a starring role. Instead she had acted like an idiot. A topless idiot – the very best sort. By tomorrow night, Ben Jones would know that she talked to her boobs and gave them names. He would know about the soup. He would have seen her half-naked. And so would everybody else. Who could she tell? Nobody. Not even Flora. Certainly not her mum.

It started to rain. Jess didn't mind. She walked on, faster and faster. The rain ran down her face. There was something soothing about it. You could cry in the rain unnoticed. Jess was sorely tempted. When she got home she was soaked. Home had never smelt so homely. She would never leave it again. Her mum had got back with Granny while Jess was at school, and Granny had the TV news on, quite loud. As Jess walked in, Granny looked up with a twinkly smile.

She switched the TV on to mute and held out her arms.

'Jess! Sweetheart! You look so grown-up! Goodness, you're wet! Have a bath straightaway, lovey, or you'll get a chill. They've found a human head in Grimsby.'

Granny's character was mostly sweet old-fashioned fussiness but with a strange lust for horror. She trawled through the newspapers for gory details of murder mysteries. If she saw a man digging his garden she immediately suspected he was burying his wife. She had watched the DVD of *Pulp Fiction* seven times, while knitting pink fluffy baby socks for the charity shop. She was, in her own loveable way, a little bit weird.

Jess's mum appeared, carrying a pile of Granny's things. She looked tired. She gave Jess a curious, expectant look.

'Hi, Mum,' said Jess. Her mum seemed very far away. Jess felt that her agony about the CCTV footage had imprisoned her in a kind of glass box. She could see ordinary life taking place out there, but she couldn't join in.

'Well . . . ?' said her mum.

'Well what?' answered Jess irritably.

'What do you think of your room?'

'Oh, Mum, it's divine! I'm so sorry! I forgot!' Jess launched herself at her mum and gave her a massive hug. 'It's the best thing that's ever happened to me! Thanks so much! You're ace! I'm going up to sort it out now. But I'm just going to have a bath first.'

Jess fled upstairs. She locked herself in the bathroom, ran a bath, jumped in, lay back and tried to relax. But her mind was whirling. How could she get her hands on that footage and destroy it for ever? Maybe she could ring Tiffany and try to bribe her. But Jess had no money, and she'd always had the impression that Tiffany didn't like her much. Jess sighed. Maybe she could feign illness and stay away from school for several days, until it had all blown over. What she needed was something huge to happen which would distract everybody from the CCTV thing. Maybe she should slip out tonight and set fire to the school. No, it would be better to set fire to Tiffany's house. Then the footage would get destroyed as well.

She poured some of her mother's oil into the bath. It was lavender – supposed to be soothing. Jess tried hard to be soothed. Setting fire to buildings was just a fantasy. Jess couldn't even light an aromatherapy candle without burning her fingers. She went back to the idea of pretending to be ill. Maybe there was an illness that lasted about a year. Surely in a year's time everybody would have forgotten all about the CCTV footage. She would have to ring her dad. He would know. He was working his way through the medical encyclopaedia. He had already got as far as D – dandruff.

'Jess!' Her mum knocked on the bathroom door. 'Fred's on the phone!'

'Tell him I'll ring him back!' called Jess. It was time to get out of the bath anyway. Her skin was going all wrinkled, like Granny's. Jess got out and dried herself. But she never said a word to Bonnie and Clyde. That kind of madness can get you into serious trouble. She hoped Bonnie and Clyde would understand, but she was afraid she wouldn't be speaking to them again for some time.

Jess rang Fred from the study. Her mum was cooking downstairs and listening to the radio in the kitchen, and Granny was still in the sitting room with the TV blasting away. Fred answered the phone.

'Hi, Mum said you rang,' said Jess.

'Yeah,' said Fred. 'I've left my copy of *Twelfth Night* in school, and I've got to finish the essay or Fothergill will rip out my intestines and turn them into a rather chic pâté. Can I come round and borrow yours?'

'Sure,' said Jess. She realised with a sickening lurch that she hadn't done her Shakespeare essay either, but her mum, being a librarian, had loads of copies of the plays, so Fred could certainly borrow her school one. Although it was covered with her lovesick graffiti about Ben Jones. She'd have to obliterate it. She didn't want Fred to see how very very doting she had been.

'What's wrong?' asked Fred. 'You're rather mono-syllabic this evening. Almost surly. Are you having a film noir moment?' Fred had just found out about film noir – those moody black and white movies of the 1940s – and he was working on an idea to reshoot *Planet of the Apes* set in post-war Paris.

'Oh, Fred, it's a disaster!' Jess blurted out. 'The CCTV footage! That party tomorrow night!'

'Oh yes,' said Fred. 'A tasteless charade, of course, but I suppose I'll have to drag myself there.'

'The thing is,' said Jess, 'I had to do some really private things in that loo – I had to like, get undressed and wash and stuff, because I'd – I'd spilt some food on myself – and everybody's going to see me naked. I can't bear it, Fred! I'll die of embarrassment! What on earth can I do?'

Fred was quiet for a moment. 'It does rather put my essay crisis into perspective,' he mused. 'My advice is, sit it out with a cool air of superior detachment and a mocking smile. Can you manage that?'

'I'll give it a try,' sighed Jess. 'Although, to be honest, I'd be more comfortable imitating a chimpanzee.'

'Well, imagine you're a chimpanzee, then,' suggested Fred. 'The great apes wouldn't care, would they? Just go through the whole evening in character – as a chimp.'

'Well, thanks a lot for the advice,' said Jess with a slight sneer. 'I wouldn't go in for a career in counselling, though, if I were you. Don't give up the day job.'

'I agree that counselling may not be my major suit,' said Fred, 'because basically I am completely self-absorbed and resent a moment of conversation spent on the problems of anybody else. I'll be round in five minutes for the Shakespeare.'

Usually Jess would have enjoyed half an hour of wisecracking and mutual character assassination with Fred, but this evening she had no appetite for it. She rang off and found her copy of *Twelfth Night*, then scribbled over all the references to Ben Jones, so that the inside of the cover was adorned with what looked like a mass of black clouds. Quite appropriate, really.

Fred came round and collected the book, and then Jess sat down and wrote the most uninspired essay ever, because all she could think about was that terrible moment which would arrive tomorrow night – when everybody she knew would see her talking to her own boobs.

Chapter 11

Jess sent Ben a text agreeing to meet him in the burger place.

'Wow! You and Ben are really getting it on!' said Flora when she heard.

Jess shrugged. Never had a date seemed less tempting. She was so nervous about the CCTV party that her appetite had completely vanished. Having a burger was out of the question. Jess feared she might never eat again. The whole business of putting objects into one's mouth and making them disappear suddenly seemed impossibly bizarre.

She did manage a hot chocolate, though. It would give her strength for the ordeal ahead. Ben sat opposite her, eating a burger and talking in his usual six-words-a-minute way.

'Have you seen *Deadly Crawlers*?' he asked.

Jess shook her head listlessly.

'It's, like, brilliant,' Ben assured her. 'It's, like, these aliens invade the earth and they kind of look like cockroaches and they can, like, shoot killer rays out of their antennae. I'll lend it to you if you like.'

Jess expressed gratitude. But she was not really listening. Sometimes, when he smiled, she managed to drag the corners of her mouth upwards in response. But it was the kind of smile an alien might have produced. Somebody trying to pass for a human. Eventually, Ben finished the last of his fries and they walked off towards Tiffany's.

Jess's legs seemed almost too heavy to walk properly. Her shoulders sagged. And though she hadn't eaten for hours and hours, her stomach seemed full of bricks.

After about ten minutes they arrived at Tiffany's.

'Cheer up,' said Ben, as they stood on the doorstep. 'It's gonna be, like, brilliant!'

That showed how much he knew. It was, in fact, going to be dire.

Tiffany opened the door and Jess stumbled in.

'Oh, hi, Jess!' said Tiffany, with a light dash of sadism. 'Jack says you're the star turn. He wouldn't let anyone else see it, so we can't wait to see what you've been up to!'

Jess smiled in what she hoped was a cool and disdainful way, and followed Tiffany down her immense hall.

They entered the palatial sitting room to vast cheers. The whole year group seemed to be here. And Tiffany's TV was, naturally, a top-of-the-range plasma job.

'Get a load of that!' whispered Ben as they sat down in a corner – which was not nearly dark enough, unfortunately. 'It's a 55-inch screen!'

Jess was unable to respond. She was just glad she was not a boy and obliged to be excited by such dull detail. She was depressed by the revelation that the TV had a 55-inch screen – so it was more than equal to the task of revealing her boobs, life-size if necessary. Jess was a mere 34A.

Across the room, Flora was sitting cuddled up to Mackenzie. She waved madly and blew kisses in an irritating way. Sitting at the back, crammed on to a sofa with about five other guys, was Fred. He pulled an ape-like face and gave her the thumbs-up sign. Jess raised an eyebrow in what she hoped was an arch and cool way, but somehow it got stuck and kind of twitched insanely, like when the satellite link stops working on the news reports. Jess turned away. She did not do a thumbs up in return. She didn't think thumbs up was a fair representation of her mood, somehow. Tiffany's brother, Jack, a rather sinister-looking guy with puppy fat, stood up and the crowd roared in approval. He raised his arms skywards.

'Enough! Enough!' he shouted. 'Let's get on with it! Nobody's seen this footage yet except me, and I can assure you, it's hot, hot, hot!'

The boys howled. The girls screamed. Jess wished she were anywhere else on earth. Oh, for the delicious joys of detention! She would rather do the washing-up for six hours than spend one more second in this hell-hole. But she just had to tough it out.

'One more thing!' cried Jack. 'We wanna tell you girls we really appreciate your being OK about this – and just to show you how grateful we are, we're gonna show you some motorsport afterwards!'

The boys joined in an animal cry of joy. The girls screamed in disgust.

'To spare your blushes,' said Jack, 'we're gonna turn down the lights. OK, Sam?'

A boy standing by the door dimmed the lights. Jess's chance had come. She dived for the 'Eject' button. But before she had even managed to touch the set, she felt herself grabbed and dragged backwards by two big boys.

'Nice try, Jordan,' commented Jack. 'Sit on her, guys.'

Harry Oakham and Joe Marks obliged. Jess could not move. She turned her face to the carpet. And closed her eyes.

Please, God, she thought, in a last-ditch attempt to escape from total shame, *help me! Send a guardian angel to arrange a power cut – anything! And I promise if you get me out of this, I'll never be a bad girl again!* It was a tall order, though, appealing for last-minute divine intervention. Knowing her luck, she'd only got through to God's voicemail.

The moment of her complete humiliation had arrived. Jess heard the DVD player whir into action. But then, there was a blare of Hollywood-type music. Jack swore. Several other boys booed. Something had gone wrong. Jess looked up and saw – to her utter amazement – the opening credits for *Snow White and the Seven Dwarfs*!

'Put the freaking lights up again!' shouted Jack, floundering about among the DVD collection – most of which was scattered about on the floor below the TV. Jack picked up DVD after DVD, examined it and chucked it aside in a desperate frenzy. 'Who's got the disc?' he demanded finally, looking up in fury, red in the face. 'Come on, whoever you are, you cretin – give it here!'

'Burn another copy,' suggested one of the boys.

'I can't, you fool,' Jack yelled. 'I had to delete the original in case my parents found it. That DVD was my only copy!'

'It's Howells!' said one of the boys. Gary Howells was pounced on, roughly searched and lightly beaten up, protesting his innocence all the while, but no disc emerged.

'Let's have the motorsport!' shouted John Woodford. 'Who wants to watch a girls' loo anyway?'

There was a howl from the boys – part anguish, part agreement. Jack looked resigned, but at least it offered him a way out.

'OK, OK,' he said. 'We can watch the CCTV later, when it turns up.'

Jess breathed a huge sigh of relief and prepared, for the first time in her life, to enjoy motorsport as it has never been enjoyed before, even by very fat men drinking lager on sofas. *Oh, thank you, thank you, God!* she thought in rapture. *Thank you, you guardian angel, whoever you are. This is the best moment of my life so far!* Only one thing bothered her. A few moments ago, she had assured God that if He got her off the hook this time, she would never be a bad girl again. It was going to be a major undertaking.

The party kind of unravelled early because watching motorsport movies wasn't the girls' idea of fun, and Jess got home by 10pm, which was fortunate, because her mum was already intensely irritated.

'I've told you, I don't approve of you going out in the evenings on weekdays!' she snapped. 'And I must know where you are!'

'I was only at Tiffany's,' grumbled Jess. 'Watching a movie. And if you really want to know, it was dead boring.'

Next day, school was buzzing with gossip. Who had nicked the disc? Rumours flew about. It had been sold to a Japanese businessman. It had been bought by satellite TV. Jack had never made it in the first place. Jess just kept her head down and her fingers crossed. OK, so yesterday she had been rescued – possibly by divine intervention. But the disc could surface at any moment and the whole CCTV party could be on again in an instant.

Jess tried immensely hard to be a good girl, as she had promised the Almighty. She didn't want to blow it by a moment's thoughtless misbehaviour. Luckily Ben Jones was absent, so she wasn't distracted from saintliness. She actually concentrated in history, and performed her set tasks in strange, neat handwriting.

She sat at the front in English and put her hand up eagerly to answer every question in a shiny virtuous voice. She ran about and attempted tennis in the sports hour, trying not to sweat too hard, as she thought God might not like it. She did not draw on her hands, doodle or daydream at all. By the end of school, she was radiantly religious and totally exhausted.

'Are you OK?' asked Flora. 'You've been a bit weird all day, babe. What is it?'

'Oh, nothing,' shrugged Jess. 'Just a headache. Got to go home early and sort my room out.'

She stomped off home on her own. The others were meeting at the Dolphin Cafe, but she didn't want to hear anything more about the blasted CCTV footage as long as she lived.

Home seemed even more of a haven than usual. It felt cosier since Granny had come to stay – possibly because she turned up the heating even in summer, and was always making cups of tea. A delightful smell drifted out from the kitchen.

'Granny's made us her famous stew,' said Jess's mum from her desk, where she was going through some bills. As she spoke, the phone rang. Jess's mum answered it, and then handed it over to Jess with an expression of grim annoyance. 'It's Fred,' she said, and walked out to the kitchen to do something domestic – perhaps to check that Granny's stew hadn't got bats and toads in it.

Jess grabbed the phone. 'Hi, Fred!' She was intrigued. Fred didn't often ring. But she was also terrified. Maybe somebody had found the disc, and Fred was ringing to warn her.

'Meet me in the bus shelter in five minutes,' said Fred briskly. 'I want to return your copy of *Twelfth Night*.'

Jess was surprised. Fred didn't usually talk in such short sentences for a start. And he'd already given her back her copy of *Twelfth Night*, at school. Something was wrong. He sounded almost sinister. Jess grabbed her jacket.

'Where are you going?' called her mum. 'Dinner's nearly ready!'

'I won't be a minute!' yelled Jess, and ran out of the house. 'I'm just going to collect my copy of *Twelfth Night* – the one Fred borrowed!'

She had on her jeans and trainers. It wasn't far to the bus shelter. It was about halfway between her house and Fred's. She ran all the way, her heart pounding with dread – and to be honest, with unaccustomed exercise. Fred was waiting there. She recognised his tall, skinny outline from afar.

'I couldn't talk on the phone,' said Fred, looking mysterious under his hood. 'My mum was listening. I thought you'd probably like to have this.' He handed over a packet wrapped in a padded bag.

'What is it?' asked Jess.

'It's the CCTV footage from Tiffany's,' said Fred. 'I got there early and nicked it yesterday when Jack was in the loo. I smuggled it out in the massive pocket in my cargoes.'

Jess fought off a terrible urge to fling her arms round Fred. She knew that was the sort of thing he hated.

'Fred – you are the best!' she cried. 'I can't tell you – I just can't tell you what this means to me.' A sudden thought occurred to her. 'Hey – you haven't actually watched it, have you?' A deep and furious blush whizzed up from the soles of her feet and enfolded her entire body.

Fred just shrugged enigmatically. 'What? Just a load of girls going to the toilet? Personally I prefer wildlife documentaries.'

Jess tried hard to work out if he was lying or not, but it was impossible with Fred.

'Just don't tell anybody it was me that took it,'

warned Fred. 'I would quite like to retain all my body parts into adulthood.'

'I swear I won't breathe a word to anybody!' vowed Jess. 'Fred, I owe you one. Tell me what I can do for you – I'll do it. I'll crawl all the way to Africa on my hands and knees and carry you back a bag of mangoes in my teeth. Say the word. I'll do it. Anything.'

'That will not be necessary,' said Fred. 'As a teenage boy, I fear and avoid fruit as the vampire avoids daylight. No need ever to mention the CCTV again. As far as I'm concerned, this never happened. Bye!' And he just turned and walked off.

Astonishing! Jess ran back home, holding on tightly to the terrible package. It wouldn't do to just fling it in a rubbish bin. She wouldn't rest till the disc had been boiled, poached, scrambled, mashed, pulverised with a mallet and drowned in boiling water. But she might just take a secret little peep at it first.

Chapter 12

Jess got back home just as her mum was placing Granny's stew on the table. Granny looked up excitedly.

'There's a man in Scotland – a tax inspector, of all people – they've discovered he murdered his wife and buried her under the barbecue!' she said.

'For goodness' sake, Granny,' said Jess's mum, 'not at the supper table! Jess – wash your hands. You can't be too careful with all this e-coli about.'

Jess put the package containing the DVD on her chair and washed her hands at the sink. They always ate in the kitchen. It was cosy, and looked out on to the garden.

'We never used to have e-coli in my day,' remarked Granny. 'Although a girl in my street did die tragically from choking on a banger.'

Granny always referred to sausages as 'bangers',

although she refused to eat them. 'I would never trust a banger as far as I could throw it,' she'd observed once, which gave Jess an idea for the Geriatric Olympics, with sausage-hurling a major event. Too bad Jess hadn't had time to organise it yet.

'What's that parcel on your chair, Jess?' asked her mum.

Jess blushed. 'Oh, just that copy of *Twelfth Night* Fred borrowed,' she said.

'Why are you blushing?' demanded her mum suspiciously.

'Is Fred your boyfriend?' asked Granny, winking playfully.

'No, Granny! He's just a mate, right? I would sooner clean the front path with my tongue than get involved with any male person in that way.'

Jess shoved the package under her chair, trying not to look furtive – trying to look as if it were, in fact, a completely uninteresting Shakespeare play.

Jess's mum ladled out the stew.

'Wow, it looks lush! I'm starving!' said Jess. 'I love Granny's stew, don't you, Mum? A positive treasure trove of savoury items.' It was important to keep talking, to distract Mum from the dreaded mysterious package.

'Oh yes!' beamed Granny. 'I don't go for this

Japanese sushi rubbish, but I love a good stew. I put a dash of oregano in it to make it more Italian this time.'

'Let's go to Italy this summer, shall we, Mum?' asked Jess. 'All three of us. They love grannies in Italy. I saw an Italian film once and it was full of grannies, all sitting in the shade and casting spells on people. Can we go to Italy, Mum? Oh pleeeeease!'

'In principle,' said her mum, sipping from a glass of water in a rather tired way, 'I'd be very interested in the idea of taking you to Italy and showing you the art treasures of the Italian Renaissance, but I'm afraid this year we're too poor.' She tucked into her stew. Phew! It seemed as if Jess's mysterious package had slipped from her mind.

'Who's your favourite Italian painter, then, Mum?'

'Botticelli,' said Jess's mum. Jess knew this already, of course. There were Botticelli paintings on every wall. Not originals, unfortunately. Jess's mum's Botticellis were all reproductions. If they'd had a Botticelli original there'd be no problem about affording to visit Italy. They'd probably have a second home there – a palace with a swimming pool.

They had *The Birth of Venus* in the bathroom. It showed a beautiful blonde girl rising up from a shell and hovering above the sea. The gods of the winds were blowing at her and a handmaiden was offering her a billowing cloak. Jess's mum had rather irritatingly remarked that Venus looked a bit like Flora.

Even more irritating was the Botticelli painting in the sitting room, because that was actually *of* Flora. Not Jess's friend Flora Barclay, obviously, but Flora the Goddess of Spring. This one also looked like Flora as well as Flora. It was quite irksome, having a friend who resembled not just one but two goddesses: the Goddess of Spring and the Goddess of Love. Especially as Jess herself was more likely to be mistaken for the ape in the famous painting *Ape with a Grape* or the dog in *Still Life with Bulldog, Salad and Fries* by Alessandro Poggibotti.

'What would you like to be goddess of, Granny?' asked Jess.

Granny thought for a minute. 'Teeth,' she replied. 'I would make sure everybody's teeth lasted a lifetime.' She sighed. 'That's what I like about stew. It just slips down. I couldn't rise to a lamb chop, these days.'

'And what would you like to be goddess of, Mum?' Jess was beginning to feel a bit more relaxed now. She was beginning to enjoy herself. She was even wondering what she herself would choose to be goddess of.

Bosoms, possibly. She would make sure everybody had massive boobs that would last a life-time. Not guys, of course. Although why not? If everybody had boobs, maybe there wouldn't be such a fuss about them. And those Sumo wrestler guys certainly –

'I'd be the Goddess of Mysterious Packages,' said Jess's mum suddenly, with a piercing stare. 'I'd have X-ray vision, so I could tell what was inside parcels without having to listen to a pack of lies.'

'You could get a job at the airport, then, dear,' said Granny. 'Although I hope you don't, because I think the libraries are safer. They haven't had any of those terrorist attacks on libraries yet, have they?'

'I'd like to see them try,' said Jess's mum with spirit. 'They wouldn't get any further than Cookery and Gardening. So, Jess: what's in your package, *really*?' She turned treacherously to her defenceless daughter.

Jess blushed again. 'I told you: *Twelfth Night*. Why are you giving me such a hard time?'

'Drugs!' said Jess's mum with a dramatic, tragic air.

'Oh, honestly, Mum! I don't touch drugs. I have never, ever tried drugs. Not even aspirin. I swear to you on . . .' Jess looked around for a sacred object, then got up from the table and walked across to the windowsill, where a copper urn had been installed, with some other bits and pieces of Granny's. 'I swear on the sacred memory of Grandpa, with his crazy hats and long nose-hair, there are no drugs in that parcel. I have never touched drugs, and I never will.' Jess placed her hand on the urn containing Grandpa's ashes.

Granny took Grandpa's ashes everywhere with her. She hadn't decided yet where to scatter them. She was always promising to. But still the urn remained. It used to be on the sideboard in her old house. Now it was on the kitchen windowsill. Not terrific in terms of hygiene, perhaps. It was bad enough having your grandparents staying with you while they were still alive. But handy when it came to swearing solemn oaths.

Jess withdrew her hand and stared defiantly at her mother. Was she going to back down and accept that there were no drugs in the package? Or was she going to insist on seeing the 'Shakespeare play'? If her mum discovered that the parcel contained instead a sinister DVD . . . If she demanded to watch it herself . . . If Jess had to witness her own mother watching the whole ghastly charade with the minestrone bra inserts . . . well, she'd die of shame. There could be another urn up there, next to Grandpa's, by the end of the week.

Chapter 13

Jess took a deep breath. There was only one way out of this. 'OK, Mum. I admit it. It's not *Twelfth Night*.'

'I know,' said her mum with a self-satisfied air. 'Because I can see *Twelfth Night* sticking out of your schoolbag over there.'

Oh no! Betrayed by her own untidiness yet again! Jess wondered whether being tidy was part of what God would regard as 'being a good girl'. If so, her chances of going to heaven were frankly nil.

'But it's not drugs, Mum. I would never be so stupid. Nor would Fred. He won't even take paracetamol. Please believe me.'

'What is it, then? And it's pointless trying to lie to me, Jess – I can see it in your face.'

'It's a DVD,' said Jess, hoping to be able to leave it at that.

'What kind of DVD? Something nasty, obviously, or you wouldn't have lied to me in the first place. Is it an adult classification one?'

'No,' said Jess.

'Is it horror?' asked Granny. 'If so, I wouldn't mind having a look. I saw a lovely one once with zombies in.'

'It's really silly,' said Jess. 'I went to a party at Tiffany's last weekend, right? Well, we found out afterwards that Tiffany's brother had rigged up a camcorder in the girls' bathroom, so every time somebody went to the loo they were on film. We were gutted, obviously. The boys organised another party – that's where I was last night. They were going to show the footage to everyone.'

'Men! Typical of the male concept of "fun"! Primitive and immature,' snapped Jess's mum.

'Yeah, right. Anyway, Fred managed to get hold of it in time and he hid it so nobody could find it yesterday. He gave it to me just now so I could destroy it.'

'Let me see it, then.' Jess's mum held out her hand.

Jess handed it over. Thank goodness she had told the truth, and not tried to pretend the DVD was about the novels of Charles Dickens or marine animals of the barrier reef. Jess's mum marched into the sitting room and shoved the DVD in the machine. Jess and

Granny followed her and sat down on the sofa. Although she had told the truth, Jess's heart was still pounding like mad. She had no idea how soon she would appear, but the thought of Mum and Granny seeing the whole charade made her want to scream aloud and run off to Borneo. Wherever Borneo was. It sounded pretty far away. Worst of all would be the revelation that she addressed her boobs as Bonnie and Clyde. Can you imagine your mum and your granny knowing that kind of stuff?

The footage kicked in with a lot of dazzle and tracking, but then it settled to a view of the bathroom at Tiffany's. You could see the washbasin and the far wall, but you couldn't actually see the loo at all – it was far over to the right, out of the picture. For a long time there was nothing at all, just the wall. It was like all CCTV footage: black and white, grainy and boring. Nobody was going to win any Oscars for this piece of cinema. *The Novels of Charles Dickens* would have been a whole lot glitzier.

Then somebody came in – a girl called Sophie whom Jess hardly knew. She marched over to the right-hand side of the screen, turned round and disappeared. You could just about tell that she was going to pull her pants down when she went out of vision.

'Well, if all the boys can come up with is this, it's a pretty poor show,' said Jess's mum, getting up. 'I've got sleazier stuff in the DVD department of the library.' And she went back to the kitchen and started clearing the plates.

Jess went on watching the footage. Sophie reappeared, pulling up her pants, came over to the washbasin and washed her hands. Then she checked her make-up, got her mascara out and reapplied it. It took ages and was very boring.

'I wish somebody would creep up and murder her,' said Granny.

'You've seen too many whodunnits, Granny,' said Jess. 'Anyway, nobody could creep up on her, unless they'd come up out of the loo.'

'That would be a good idea,' said Granny. 'A murderer in a wet-suit, wielding a harpoon.'

'You'd never get the harpoon round the S-bend, Granny,' Jess pointed out. She was beginning to feel better. But she still wished Granny would go to bed.

Sophie finally finished her make-up and left the bathroom. There was another long wait. Then Alice Andrews came in, took out her contact lenses, rinsed them, put them in again and used some eye drops. Then she blew her nose. Then she washed her hands.

Then she started looking for something in her bag. Then she looked in the mirror again and went out.

'I'm getting a bit bored with this, Jess, love,' said Granny. 'Can't we watch the latest James Bond instead?'

Jess wanted to see more of the tape, but she didn't want Granny to see it. She had no way of knowing how many girls had visited the loo before her. She might appear on screen any moment with minestrone all over her cleavage.

'OK, Granny.' Jess put on James Bond for Granny, but went off upstairs with the DVD. She told Granny she had work to do – which was true. She still hadn't started her latest essay. However, once upstairs, she was distracted by the chaotic grandeur of her new bedroom. Her stuff lay strewn everywhere, spilling out of black plastic sacks. She should have sat down at the desk and started to plan an essay entitled 'Shakespeare's *Twelfth Night* may be a comedy, but it also has darker moments'. Instead she started sorting her clothes out, folding them up and putting them carefully in the drawers. It was virtually the first time in her life she had done this kind of thing, but it was sort of enjoyable in a weird, perverted kind of way.

Her mum knocked on her door half an hour later.

'I'm sorry I didn't believe you about the DVD, darling,' she said, and gave Jess a hug. 'I'm a little bit stressed out today. Anyway, Granny's going to bed now – can you just pop down and kiss her goodnight?'

'Sure,' said Jess. She ran downstairs and kissed Granny, who was sitting up in bed in what had once been Jess's room. It didn't seem anything like it used to be. Even the bed was in a different place.

'Jess,' whispered Granny, 'would you mind bringing Grandpa in here with me? I don't like to be separated from him, in case I go in my sleep.' She winked roguishly. For somebody who thought about death all the time, Granny was amazingly cheerful.

Jess brought the urn in from the kitchen windowsill and placed it on Granny's bedside table.

'I'm going to throw him into the sea one day, if I'm spared, dear,' confided Granny. 'But if I go before I get round to it, will you promise to do it for me? It's a little place down in Cornwall, where we spent our honeymoon. It's called Mousehole.'

Jess promised, though of course she reassured Granny that she looked exceptionally healthy and would certainly live till she was a hundred.

'I don't want your mum to have custody of Grandpa,'

explained Granny conspiratorially. 'She would probably just chuck him on her carrot patch.'

Jess assured Granny that she would prevent her mother from top-dressing the vegetable plot with the remains of either grandparent, and eventually managed to get away. She ran upstairs to get the DVD.

'Jess!' called her mum as she passed the door of the box room. 'I'm absolutely shattered, I'm going to bed early. Will you make sure all the lights are out when you go to bed, love? But leave the one on in the hall downstairs, in case Granny wants to go to the loo in the night.'

Jess nodded, kissed her mum, and then went back downstairs to see the rest of the footage. She fast-forwarded through the boring bits, but she saw some things that surprised her. Two girls came in together, for a start. Shona Miles and Lily Thornton. Shona did her hair while Lily went to the loo. Fancy having a pee while somebody else was in the room! Jess knew that Shona and Lily were inseparable buddies, but she would never, ever, ever have peed in front of Flora. She had heard that in India people just peed and pooed in the street. Well, she was never going to do that. She didn't even like having paintings of people in the loo. Their eyes always followed you around the room, with a kind of mocking look.

Anyway, Lily and Shona were soon off the screen, and somebody else charged in and disappeared off the screen on the other side. It was Donna Fielding, evidently desperate for the loo. She didn't wash her hands when she'd finished, either.

'Disgusting!' cried Jess. She would certainly never have lunch at Donna's ever again.

After Donna, Jodie Gordon came in, and embarked on a massive spot-squeezing exercise that went on and on and on – her chin, her brow, her shoulders, even the tops of her boobs. Jess watched in fascinated horror. Eventually Jodie finished, pulled a face at the mirror, said something, sneered at her reflection and left.

It was getting late and, fascinating though all this was, Jess had become impatient for her own performance. She fast-forwarded through the footage until the awful moment when she herself appeared. Jess recognised her own image with a gasp of horror. But she ran across the screen and disappeared on the side where the loo was. The removing of the bra inserts and throwing them down the loo was completely out of view.

She came over to the wash-basin and pulled off her top. The washing of her boobs was certainly the high point of the tape so far, but it didn't last long – she soon turned her back, dried herself, and got dressed again. And though you could see her lips move, there was no soundtrack, so nobody would know her terrible secret – that she talked to her boobs, and called them Bonnie and Clyde.

Jess ejected the disc, and went into the kitchen. She could hear Granny snoring faintly in her room. There was no sound from her mum upstairs. Jess wondered how to destroy the DVD. She filled the washing-up bowl with water and immersed the disc in it. Then she took it out, put it on the floor, and stamped on it. Then she picked up the shattered, dripping remnants and stuffed them in the rubbish bin.

Lying in bed later, she felt that it hadn't been as bad as she'd feared. Nobody would know about the minestrone. Nobody would know about Bonnie and Clyde. True, she had appeared topless. But she'd rather be seen topless than squeezing her spots like Jodie.

And there was something strangely reassuring about her appearance. Bonnie and Clyde weren't nearly as tiny as she had thought. OK, she was never going to be famous for a massive bust. She was always going to be able to see her feet and get through turnstiles. There was no danger of her knocking priceless china ornaments off a shelf just by turning round. But Bonnie and Clyde were, well, adequate. And though Jack, and possibly some of his mates, had seen the footage, she didn't care, because they were older and she didn't really know them. The main thing was Ben Jones hadn't seen it. Or Mackenzie.

As for Fred, well, he'd said he hadn't watched it. He'd said he'd rather watch wildlife documentaries. Was that true? You could never tell, with Fred. Jess wasn't sure if she'd mind if Fred had seen it or not. One thing was certain: he had performed a heroic act in getting the disc to her. She owed him one. But she wasn't exactly sure one *what*.

Chapter 14

'Whoever nicked that DVD is a totally brainless idiot,' Mackenzie said.

He and Ben and Flora and Jess were sitting on the wall outside the science block at break. They were still talking about the CCTV. But now, at last, Jess was OK about it, because she knew it would never be found. She had got a guardian angel, and his name was Fred Parsons. An unexpected name for an angel, but life was like that.

'Jack said that tape was dynamite. Ace. Wicked. We could've cashed in, big time,' said Mackenzie.

'Speaking as one of the so-called stars of this rather sordid little charade,' snapped Jess, 'I'd be grateful to anyone who was idiot enough to destroy it.'

'No need to be so touchy,' said Flora. She didn't like it when Jess snapped at Mackenzie. 'It's only a bit of fun.'

'You wouldn't think it was only a bit of fun if you'd been in that bathroom, doing private stuff on camera!' Jess turned on Flora.

Flora frowned, looked away and sighed, as if Jess was being tiresome and childish. Jess scowled and glared at the horizon, because Flora definitely *was* being tiresome and childish, as well as being on the side of the boys, which was the worst betrayal of all. Ben Jones looked admiringly at his trainers. He hadn't spoken for ten minutes. Yes, they were a happy little foursome.

Suddenly Ben turned to Mackenzie. 'Um, what extras are there on your dad's new PC?' he said.

Mackenzie looked relieved. They plunged into a geeky discussion about computers.

Typical! thought Jess. *Can't cope with emotion.*

'Strange how males like to escape into technology,' observed Jess. 'The only one I know who doesn't is Fred.'

Although her own dad hadn't a clue about technology either, and when his car once broke down he had begged and pleaded with it to start again instead of masterfully plunging into the engine and redwonking the piston flagelongas. 'Please, please, Ada, I beg you! Be a good girl and start for me and I'll give you a lovely new can of oil for your supper tonight!' he had said. Then, when Ada had refused to start, he had shouted, 'You traitor! We're finished!' And got out and kicked the car's side. Jess realised, however, that her dad was a bit unusual in this respect. He was, after all, an artist.

'You have to admit Fred is a bit weird,' said Flora.

'Weird?' snapped Jess. 'What's weird about him? Original and brilliant, possibly, and if that's your idea of weird – well, stick with mediocrity if it makes you feel more at home.'

Flora frowned. She wasn't fiery-tempered like Jess. But she always argued like a dog with a bone, gnawing away stubbornly and never letting go.

'Well, he is a bit of a loner, isn't he? And the way he talks – like he thinks he's Mr Darcy or something. And you're always trying to copy him.'

'I do NOT try and copy him!' exploded Jess. Ben and Mackenzie twitched nervously.

'Do you rate Goth War Final Destruct?' enquired Mackenzie. They were on to computer games now.

Ben thought for a minute. 'Yeah, but not in the same league as, well, um – Black Lords Search and Destroy.'

'Well, since most boys seem to prefer talking like robots,' observed Jess icily, 'somebody who talks like Mr Darcy ought to be given a medal, not treated as a fool.' She got up off the wall and walked away, seething.

She hated the way Flora always seemed to take sides with the boys. Filming girls in the bathroom wasn't a bit of fun; it was an invasion of their privacy. But it was all right for Flora – she'd escaped unscathed, as usual. Protected by the guardian angel who seemed to watch over all blonde high-achievers with perfect rich families, Flora had miraculously not wanted to pee.

All through French, Jess brooded. She sat on the other side of the room from Flora, and at change of lessons ignored her and walked quickly away. In her head, she rehearsed a scene in which Miss Jessica Jordan drew up in her coach outside a muddy hovel. She wound the window down – or whatever you did with coach windows – and peered contemptuously out.

Miss Flora appeared at the door of the hovel, her head hanging in shame, her clothes in rags.

'Forgive me, dear Miss Jordan!' she cried, and threw herself to the ground. 'I was mistaken. Sir Frederick is a man of exemplary character. I was misled by the attentions of other gentlemen. Forgive me, I pray!'

'Do not humiliate yourself so much,' observed Miss Jessica Jordan crisply. 'It is not becoming. Here is a sovereign. Pray

*go to the baths to repair your appearance, and buy yourself
a modest gown of grey wool. Antoine – drive on!'*

*She tossed the coin on to the ground. Miss Jordan's coach
bowled off into the distance, whilst Miss Flora scrabbled in
the cloud of dust for the sovereign.*

Geography was particularly dull. They were studying
the coalfields of Pittsburgh. This just added to Jess's
bad temper. Why, with the whole glorious world at
their disposal, did geography teachers always choose
coalfields and marshes to talk about? Why didn't they
talk about rainforests full of monkeys or South Sea
islands, with strips of dazzling sand and coconut palms?
Jess was supposed to be making a list of coalfields in
North America – an activity so dull as to be a non-
chemical alternative to sleeping pills. Instead she made
a list of reasons why she hated Flora. It went like this:

1. Great beauty and no fatty bits: slim and yet large
    boobs (unfair!)
2. Great wealth
3. Great intelligence: straight As in every subject
4. Mother also tactlessly beautiful: has probably had
    a facelift
5. Parents not divorced, but appear to be happily
    married (aliens possibly?!)

6. Father rich and masterful. Would never shout at his car, and it's a Mercedes
7. Their car would never break down (see above)
8. Several bathrooms, all with gold taps
9. Have to take shoes off in her house as if it's a mosque
10. Boys all look at her and drool like very large dogs looking at a bone

At this point Mr Chapman unexpectedly asked Jess to read out her list of coalfields.

After detention, Jess walked out of school with the deepest of depressions draped over her shoulders like a coat of lead. But there, waiting for her, were Flora and Jodie Gordon, spot queen of the CCTV footage.

'Jess!' cried Flora. 'I'm so so sorry! I was so horrible! I so hate it when we have a row! I've got you a chocolate bar and some Pepsi and I'm gonna give you my stripy top – the one you like in black and gold. Please forgive me!'

OK, she wasn't actually grovelling in the dust, in rags, but it was a handsome apology. And Jess was starving.

They hugged each other and got stuck into the chocolate. Jodie had some mini eclairs, so it was a real choc fest.

'I was caught on that film as well,' Jodie said. 'I've just been telling Flora. I went in there and squeezed my spots for hours. If they'd showed it to everybody I'd have died! Boys are just pigs and we should never split up because of them!'

'Yeah, boys are the enemy!' agreed Flora.

Jess thought of all the good times she and Flora had had since they first met years ago. Jodie was right. It was crazy for girls' friendships to be ruined by mere beings from Mars – aliens.

They walked off arm in arm, all three of them. There's nothing like chocolate for cheering you up.

'Boys are animals,' said Jodie. Her mother was a feminist, too.

'Yeah,' agreed Jess. 'For a start, Carter is an elephant. Although that is rather unkind to elephants. And Whizzer is a gorilla – although he lacks the gorilla's high I.Q.'

'What about Ben Jones?' said Flora teasingly.

Jess gritted her teeth. 'He reminds me of a certain kind of camel,' she said fearlessly. 'And as for Mackenzie, he's one of those bushbaby things that comes out at night. With very endearing faces and curly fur, but a horrid ferocious bite.'

Flora looked relieved. It seemed her sweetheart had got off lightly.

'And what about Jack?' asked Jodie.

Jess thought about Tiffany's brother, he who had had the idea of setting up the bathroom camera in the first place.

'He's a vile loathsome poisonous tarantula spider,' said Jess. 'He even has black hairy legs – I saw them last summer at the pool. It appeared he had only two, but I bet the other six were folded away in his swimming shorts.'

'And what about Mr Chapman?'

'Mr Chapman is a donkey.' The geography teacher did indeed have grey hair, a worn-out expression and a very loud and bizarre laugh.

'And what about my dad?' asked Flora.

Jess took care over this one. 'Your dad is the king of the beasts,' said Jess diplomatically. 'The lion, of course.'

'And what about your dad?' asked Flora.

Jess thought fondly of her male parent: his nervousness, his long thin legs, his startled look, his fondness for fish. 'My dad's a heron.'

'And what about Fred?' asked Jodie.

Jess thought about Fred: his strange solitary behaviour, his wisdom, his addiction to violent films.

'Fred's an owl,' she said. 'I can just see him tearing

the heads off rats every night. In fact, for all we know, that's precisely how he spends his leisure hours.'

Jess and Flora said goodbye to Jodie and then trudged on, finishing the chocolate. Minutes after getting back from school, Jess was curled up on her sofa with Flora, watching MTV and eating pizza. This was the life!

'I'm so glad we're friends again, Jess. I just couldn't cope without you,' said Flora. 'And it's so great that Ben and you are getting it together.'

'We aren't,' said Jess.

'But he asked you to have coffee at the cafe!' insisted Flora. 'And the burger bar! And you two came to the CCTV party together.'

'That doesn't mean anything,' said Jess. 'I think he just hangs around with me because Mackenzie's always busy with you these days.'

'Oh no!' said Flora. 'He's crazy about you, anyone can see that. He's just a bit shy. All he needs is the right moment. He's probably a bit self-conscious about making a move in public. I bet he's waiting till he gets you on your own, without other people in your face all the time.'

Jess wondered if this were true. She certainly hoped so. That night in bed, Jess enjoyed a delicious fantasy in which Ben Jones hired a balloon and floated away with her over the countryside in perfect, total peace and privacy. She hoped God wouldn't mind. Although now she knew that it was Fred who had rescued her, she had gone back to being a bit uncertain about whether or not she believed in God. One thing was for sure – she certainly believed in Fred. He was her guardian angel. Or something. Bless his long straggly locks!

Chapter 15

A few days later, Fred sidled up to Jess after English. The room was empty, as Mr Fothergill had lumbered off to perform some gross act in the privacy of the staffroom, possibly involving the tea urn and powdered milk. The rest of the class had similarly evaporated at speed. Flora and Mackenzie had rushed off together to find a private place in which to admire each other's earlobes and eyelashes. Ben had gone off to a football practice. Only Jess was left, because she still hadn't quite finished her essay about dark moments in *Twelfth Night*. 'Although *Twelfth Night* is a comedy,' Mr Fothergill had announced, 'it does have its dark moments. Rather like life. Ha ha!'

'Er . . . any chance you can do me a favour?' said Fred.

'A favour?' cried Jess. 'After what you did for me?

Name it! I trust it will involve considerable pain and inconvenience.'

'Well, yes, of course,' said Fred. 'Otherwise it wouldn't be worth asking.'

'OK, then – reveal my ordeal,' Jess said, grinning.

Fred sat down on an adjoining desk and sort of played with his long scruffy locks of hair.

'I do wish you'd have your hair cut, by the way,' said Jess.

'Yeah, yeah,' sighed Fred. 'I'm waiting for the right moment. Anyway, the deal is, it's my mum's birthday tomorrow.'

'Oh! I adore your mum! She is appallingly delightful!'

'Yes, well . . .' Fred frowned a bit. 'I don't know what to get her. Could you possibly buy her some small token of my affection – some female-type thing, possibly adorned with lace and rosebuds? If anyone saw me buying something like that, my street cred would be at an end for ever.' He took a crumpled twenty pound note from his pocket. 'Be lavish,' he said. 'And . . .' He hesitated, and blushed a little.

Jess was intrigued. What was coming? A guarded reference to lingerie?

'Well, we're having a little birthday-type tea round about six tomorrow, and she said I could bring a friend as long as it was you. Sorry to impose such a night-mare on you, but it will keep the old bat happy.' He shrugged, and looked at Jess with his head cocked on one side and his eyes sort of shining.

'It's not a nightmare, you plonker! It'll be ace!' cried Jess. 'I so love your mum! I'll be there, glamorous present in hand!'

'OK, and – well, don't, like, mention it to anybody, yeah?' Fred got up. 'Not even to Flora. She'd only tell Mackenzie and . . . I don't want everybody to know.'

'Of course!' said Jess. She was really looking forward to it. She had felt so happy in Fred's house. And she was already planning to get Fred's mum something really stunning. Twenty pounds! Fred must have been saving up, or maybe he'd raided his piggy bank, because Fred was famously always broke.

'Gotta go now – chess club.' Fred sidled off towards the door and briefly imitated a chimpanzee before disappearing with a strange ape-like cry. Jess returned to her essay about dark moments. Sunlight flooded the room. For once, her own life didn't seem all that dark. She had come through the CCTV ordeal, and now things were steaming along nicely. Fred's mum had invited her to her birthday party! How unbelievably sweet! Jess hoped there would be chocolate cake.

It was no problem, next day, keeping it a secret.

'Doing anything after school, Jess?' asked Flora at break.

'No, just going to whizz off home,' said Jess. 'Mum's at a librarians' conference in Oxford and she won't be back till late. So I've got to get back and keep Granny in order. Otherwise she might escape and go out on a spree, mugging young men.' This was partly true, in fact. Jess's mum *was* at a conference and she had asked Jess to check on Granny straightaway after school – but Jess reckoned that she'd still have time to get Fred's mum a glamorous present and turn up at six o'clock for the birthday tea.

Jess didn't mention Fred's mum's party to Flora, though. She would have kept it secret even if Fred hadn't asked her to. If Flora knew that shopping for presents was involved, she would certainly hijack the event, and possibly tag along in an irritating way, and get invited in. Then it would be the work of a moment for Flora to fascinate Fred's mum and replace Jess in that lovely woman's fickle heart.

'Yeah, I've gotta go home straightaway, too,' sighed Flora. 'My dad is being, like, so hard on me about Mackenzie. Anyone would think Mac was a drug dealer or something, rather than a small furry animal.'

Jess rather wished Flora would keep details of her love life to herself, even though it was Jess who had compared Mackenzie to a small furry animal in the first place.

Morning school was uneventful. Jess was in a happy dream, trying to decide whether to buy Fred's mum some delectable bath items in what seemed to be her favourite spicy range, or some perfume, or maybe a fabulous pair of earrings. She had a whole two and a half hours after school to nip home, make sure Granny was OK, then zoom into town on the bus and ransack the department stores and chic little boutiques. What a delightful evening this was going to be! Possibly the best this year. Nothing on earth could spoil it. Could it?

Chapter 16

The bell rang for the end of school, and Jess was out of the blocks like a sprinter whose last chance had come for an Olympic gold. She dashed home. She would spend ten seconds reassuring Granny, making sure she had her glasses, her hearing aid, the TV remote, a pile of lovely food and a blood-curdling murder mystery to read. Then Jess could quickly get changed (another ten seconds – no, say twenty, maybe) and dash off to the city centre for an hour's frenzied shopping. She would buy Fred's mum the best present ever, not counting an actual live puppy.

However, as Jess arrived home and pushed the front door open, she saw something strange. The hall floor was sort of shining and moving. Oh my goodness! It was covered in water! Hastily Jess removed her shoes and socks. There was a horrid cascading sound, some-where in the kitchen.

'Granny?' called Jess, splashing along the hall. 'Granny?' There was no answer. Jess's heart missed a beat.

She reached the kitchen. A tap was running: the kitchen sink had overflowed, and was still overflowing, a continuous curtain of water cascading on to the floor. Thank heavens Granny was not lying on the floor, drowned. Jess had heard somewhere that you could drown in a saucer of water if you were really unlucky – or really determined. She turned off the tap, and the waterfall sound began to slow down and become a little less like Niagara.

'Granny?' Jess called, splashing back towards Granny's room.

A terrible fear seized her. Maybe Granny had turned on the tap, then felt a bit ill and sat down and died in her chair. She would still be sitting there like a waxwork, with her eyes kind of horribly open. It would be just like Granny to die with maximum ghoulish panache. Jess peeped round the door of Granny's room. It was empty. Except for a sea of water swilling about on the floor, ankle deep. Granny's knitting pattern, which had been on the floor by her chair, was floating about. Where on earth was she, though? Had she gone upstairs to escape the rising waters?

'Granny! Granny?' yelled Jess, racing upstairs. She looked everywhere. Nothing. No aged person. Only Rasputin looking startled and disapproving. 'Where's Granny, Rasputin? For goodness' sake! Have you eaten her?'

Rasputin looked shocked and innocent. Jess paused, her mind whirling.

This was a disaster. Her mum had left her in charge and she had somehow lost Granny and flooded the house! What should she do? Should she ring the police, or was that overreacting? What if Granny had just decided to go for a walk? The police would be really cross. Although going for a walk on her own was not really Granny's style, what with her bad knee and everything.

Suddenly, the phone rang in her mum's study. Jess picked it up.

'Jess? This is Mrs Phillips next door. Your grandmother is round here with us. She locked herself out earlier so we took her in until you came back from school.'

'Is she OK?' asked Jess.

'Oh, yes, she's fine!' said Mrs Phillips. 'We'll bring her back round, now you're home.'

Jess rang off, went downstairs and splashed her way to the front door. The flood water had gone down a bit, but it was still total chaos.

She opened the door just as Granny was coming up the path, accompanied by Mrs Phillips and several of her irritating small children.

'Here we are!' beamed Mrs Phillips.

Granny looked embarrassed. 'The wind blew the front door shut, dear! How can I have been so silly?' She shook her head in disbelief. 'I only went out to take something to the dustbin.' Then Granny caught sight of the flooded hall. 'High cockalorum!' she cried in alarm (this was Granny's emergency swearword). 'What on earth's happened?'

'Please can we paddle? Please can we paddle?' cried the awful Phillips children. 'Mum! Can I get my boat? Can we get Laura's duck?'

'No, no, be quiet, stand still!' said Mrs Phillips. She always grinned foolishly when her children behaved like savages. Jess had babysat for them once and they had thrown a giraffe at her and waved their bare bottoms in her face. Never again. 'Oh dear, I wish I could help!' said Mrs Phillips. 'Only Archie needs changing,' she brandished a stinking baby, 'and Arabella will be waking up from her nap any minute now.'

'We can manage!' said Jess firmly. 'Wait there, Granny! I'll get you some wellies!'

'Is there a burst pipe or something? Should you call a plumber?' asked Mrs Phillips, trying to hold back her revolting offspring.

'No, it was just a tap left on,' said Jess, returning with the wellies, which had escaped the flood, being in a heap of stuff on a shelf on the hall stand.

'Oh no!' cried Granny. 'I remember now! I was just about to do the washing-up! I turned the tap on and I just popped out to take the rubbish bag to the dustbin – and there was a gust of wind, and the door slammed shut behind me!'

'It's fine, Granny – it won't take me a minute to mop it up!' insisted Jess, helping Granny into the wellies.

'Well, good luck!' said Mrs Phillips.

Granny thanked her graciously for providing emergency accommodation, but looked relieved as the Phillips clan moved off down the path, the children wailing in disappointment.

Jess took Granny's arm, as the hall floor was quite slippery, even in wellies. She escorted her to her own room.

'Those children are an absolute menace, dear,' confided Granny. 'I'm afraid there were moments when I contemplated infanticide. Oh dear! My poor rugs! I bought those in the Lake District in 1973!'

'They should feel completely at home, then!' joked Jess. But for once Granny did not laugh. She just sat there looking rather pale and distressed. Jess decided to put on the DVD of *Pulp Fiction*. That would cheer Granny up.

It seemed the electricity hadn't been affected – maybe the sockets were too high up the wall to be damaged, or something – anyway, soon Jess had settled Granny down with a cup of tea, a toasted sandwich and John Travolta brandishing a loaded gun.

Then Jess embarked on the massive task of mopping up. First she opened the back door and swept out all the water on the kitchen floor. This area was going to be easy, because it was ceramic tiles. Then she opened the front door and swept all the remaining water out of the hall. Next she started on the mop-and-bucket routine – in Granny's room, first. Jess took the two sacred Lake District rugs out and hung them on the washing line in the back garden.

Granny's carpet was still sopping wet. Jess ran upstairs and fetched a pile of dry bath towels. Mopping up Granny's floor with these seemed to work a treat. Soon the carpet was just damp rather than soaked.

'God bless you, dear, you are a good girl!' exclaimed Granny, turning away from her beloved bloodshed for a split second.

Jess returned to the kitchen and worked her way right across the kitchen floor with the mop and bucket, and then down the hall.

She was halfway down the hall when the front door-bell rang. What now? If it was those wretched kids from next door, Jess might just scream at them. She opened the door with her mouth open and a terrible frown, just in case. But it wasn't the Phillips children. It was Ben Jones, carrying a sports bag and holding a DVD. He took in the whole panorama: Jess frowning, wet, dishevelled, barefoot and wielding a dirty mop.

'Are you OK?' he asked.

'We've had a flood,' Jess explained. 'It's OK. I'm dealing with it.'

'I've got to get to football practice,' said Ben, look-ing awkward. 'Otherwise I'd give you a hand, yeah?'

'It's fine, it's OK, I've done most of it,' Jess assured him.

'I just dropped by to lend you that film, yeah?' Ben handed it over. 'I told you about it? The insects with, like, antennae that can shoot death rays?'

'Oh, yeah!' Jess remembered something of the kind

from their conversation in the burger bar. 'Brilliant, thanks.' It would be impolite to mention how much she hated insects. And, indeed, death rays.

Suddenly Ben's mobile rang.

'Hi, yeah?' he said. 'Sure – I'm on my way. I'm at Jess Jordan's – I'll be there in five minutes . . . OK, OK. No need to hassle.' He rang off. 'Whizzer getting steamed up cos I'm late.' He shook his head and grinned. 'Gotta go. Enjoy the DVD. And . . . good luck with the – you know.' He gestured towards the wet hall floor as he backed off down the path.

Jess waved goodbye and shut the front door. My goodness! Had she ever looked such a mess?

Jess ran to the mirror in the downstairs cloakroom. She looked like some kind of hideous sea otter who had just gone ten rounds with a killer whale. Ben Jones would never fancy her now. In fact, nobody would. Except possibly some eccentric fisherman from the Outer Hebrides. Jess wondered where the Outer Hebrides were, because she just might choose to go and start a new life there as her old life seemed to have reached a complete and utter dead end.

Jess sighed, took Ben's DVD into the sitting room and placed it on the shelf.

'Who was that, dear?' asked Granny.

'Just a friend of mine, Granny. He lent me a film.'

'That nice boy you like, who always lends you films, dear? What's his name? Fred?'

'Oh no – Fred!' Jess gasped. 'I totally forgot! I'm supposed to be going to his mum's birthday party! What time is it?'

Granny squinted, with agonising slowness, at her twinkly watch.

'Twenty to seven, dear,' she announced, eventually.

Twenty to seven? She was already forty minutes late! Jess ran out and raced upstairs, not so much to get ready – it was far too late for that – but to have a nervous breakdown in private.

Upstairs, Jess rushed into her mum's study and hesitated by the phone. She hadn't bought the present! She hadn't rung to say she was going to be late! She was wet through and filthy – it would take half an hour at the very least to make herself look respectable. She needed a bath, clean clothes – she'd have to wash her hair . . . and dry it . . .

Jess faced the awful truth. There was no way she was going to make it to Fred's mum's party. She had totally and utterly blown it. She must ring them and explain. She reached for the phone. Then she hesitated. It seemed such a stupid excuse.

'My granny left the tap running.' 'I had to mop up some water.' *Oh, for goodness' sake*, she thought, *get a life! Or at least get an excuse that works.* Jess felt sick with horror. Sick, sick, sick.

That was it! She'd say she was ill! Hastily she dialled Fred's number. Her heart was thudding away so fast, it felt as if it might explode.

'Yes?' said a voice. It was Fred's.

'Oh, Fred! I'm so sorry!' gasped Jess. 'I've been really, really ill! I've been sick like sort of non-stop ever since I got home! I've been, like, lying on the bathroom floor by the loo for hours! I didn't even dare to come to the phone till now!'

There was a silence from the other end. Jess cringed. Her story had sounded so transparently a lie.

'Oh well,' said Fred, rather coldly. 'Never mind. We'll start without you.'

So they'd been waiting for her! Oh no! Sort of sitting around sweetly feeling embarrassed and look-ing at the clock!

'Oh, Fred, I'm so terribly terribly sorry!' Jess was almost sobbing now. 'And you haven't got a present for your mum or anything. I've really let you down. I'm so sorry!'

'It's OK,' said Fred. 'It's fine. Get well soon.' But he

sounded hurt. Fred would normally never just use two or three words when a hundred were available.

'I hope you have a really great party, anyway,' said Jess forlornly. How she longed to be there.

'Sure. OK. Bye!' Fred rang off and was replaced by a horrid electronic buzz.

Jess ran into her room and threw herself face down on her bed.

'Oh, Rasputin! I've totally blown it!' she sobbed. 'I've let Fred down in the worst possible way! I've ruined his mum's birthday! And he's all cold and hurt!'

Rasputin looked startled, but he stroked her cheek with his velvety paws. 'Cry on my shoulder, me dear, help yourself,' he seemed to say. 'After all, that's what we teds are for.'

Jess burst into tears, seized Rasputin and cried and cried and cried and cried and cried and cried and cried and cried and cried. And cried. Bitterly. And then she cried some more. Rasputin had to be placed on a radiator afterwards, where he steamed gently for some time.

Chapter 17

Later that evening, Jess's mum came back from Oxford, and Granny went into raptures about how heroic Jess had been, dealing with the flood. Her mum came up to Jess's room to tell her how pleased she was. It was obvious Jess had been crying.

'What's the matter, love?' asked her mother gently.

Jess shrugged. 'Nothing,' she said. 'Just felt a bit upset by it all.'

'You've been brilliant!' said her mum, and gave her a hug. 'I'll take you into town at the weekend and we'll do some clothes shopping!'

Jess ought to have been grateful. She knew her mum hated clothes shopping only slightly less than she hated war. But Jess couldn't think any further ahead than school tomorrow. How on earth was she ever going to be able to make it up to Fred? And why had she told that stupid lie about being sick? She wanted to confide in her mum, but she knew if she did, her mum would want to sort it out for her. She might even ring Fred's mum and discuss the whole thing at horrible length. Jess cringed at the thought of her mother still trying to organise her social life for her. This was her mess, and she'd sort it out herself. If, indeed, it could be sorted.

Fred hadn't shouted at her. He had been much too furious for that. A couple of polite words, and then he had hung up on her. She was desperate to see him. She just had to apologise, explain and think of ways to make it up to him. Until she'd made it up with him, she'd never be able to think about anything else.

Morning lessons were science and maths, which added another sort of anguish to Jess's situation. She was in a different maths set from Fred, and as she hadn't seen him yet, she would have to wait till lunchtime and try to track him down in the library. Normally, the library was a delightful sanctuary: warm in winter and cool in summer. It was also quite dark. One's spots were not too obvious. It smelt quaintly of books, unlike the gym, for instance, which smelt of sweaty pants.

Mrs Forsyth was in charge of the library, and boy, was she fierce. There was a serious 'No Eating, No

Talking' rule. Just spending half an hour in such a strict atmosphere became a kind of secret gameshow. Trying to snack unobserved was a major challenge, especially if it involved crisps or cheesy biscuits. You had to summon up a huge amount of saliva for a start, slip the crisp into your mouth while pretending to scratch your nose, and soak the crisp in spit for about a minute before daring to risk a chomp.

You could only chew when Mrs Forsyth was not looking in your direction – and she had the eyesight of an eagle and the hearing of a spy satellite. She could hear people eating crisps in China. Jess's greatest triumph had been to open a bottle of Pepsi under the table, while Fred blotted out the '*FFFFFFophphphsttttt!*' sound with an attack of dramatic death-bed coughing. Fred and Jess had had some great illegal lunches there. But would they ever again? Or were they finished as a double act for ever?

When the bell went for lunch, Flora appeared.

'I've told Mackenzie and B.J. we'll meet them in the gym gallery,' she said. 'How are you getting on with Ben? Whizzer says Ben was at your place last night. That's why he was late for football practice. So what's going on?'

Flora was grinning – like an idiot. But Jess didn't

want to tell her anything about it. Revealing what a disaster it had been would mean that Jess had to relive the whole painful story. Instead she would tantalise Flora by revealing absolutely nothing.

'He dropped by to lend me a DVD,' she snapped. 'It was a major non-event.'

Flora's face changed. Jess could read her disappointment.

'Let's go to the gym gallery, anyway,' said Flora hastily. 'They'll be waiting for us.'

The gym gallery had so little going for it. Down in the gym various vain sporty types would be working on their six-packs and polishing their pectorals, while up in the gallery their hordes of fans gawped and drooled: girls whose brains had been replaced by marshmallow. Jess told Flora she would rather be turned into dog biscuits and fed to an elderly German Shepherd with saliva overload than spend five minutes in the gym gallery.

It suited Jess for Flora to go off there, however. Jess wanted to be alone in her attempt to find Fred in the library and apologise to him. If he wasn't there, at least being in the library would offer therapy. Jess would find a book with some male nudes in it and draw hide-ous faces on their rude bits. Her favourite was one of the biology books which had a page called 'Physical Changes at Puberty'.

It showed what seemed to be a family group: a girl of about ten, a girl of about fifteen, a woman in her thirties, and two boys and a man of similar ages. As they were all stark naked, there was something understandably embarrassed about the way they were sort of standing in a line with all their rude bits just flapping about: as if they were queuing at a supermarket checkout in a naturist resort. Jess had rescued the girls and women by drawing in tasteful black bikinis, but made the boys and the man look even more foolish by colouring their rude bits violent neon colours and adorning them with strange hairs, warts and spiders' webs.

Jess entered the library, and her heart leapt as she spotted Fred in his usual place. She headed straight for his table. She would sit down and write a note saying, *Please come outside for a minute so I can express the huge, huge regret I feel about yesterday*. But then something awful happened. Fred, who had looked up as she had come through the library doors, suddenly got to his feet, quickly replaced the book he had been reading and marched past her and out of the library without even catching her eye. He totally blanked her.

Jess was suddenly aware of people watching. She did her best not to betray her horror. She acted as if nothing unusual had happened. She selected a place near where he had been sitting, pretended to scan the shelves and chose a book at random. She opened it and stared at it, and absent-mindedly unscrewed her pen, as if she were thinking of making some notes. But all the time she was praying, *Oh please, please, make him stop being angry with me*. But was God listening? Or was He relaxing on the sofa with a beer, having switched on His answerphone?

Maybe she should write a letter to Fred: a crawling, imploring apology offering him her services as slave for life if he would forgive her. She found a piece of paper, but did not write *Dear Fred* in case anyone casually walking past saw it. Suddenly the library doors swung open. Jess prayed that it was Fred coming back in. But it was only Jodie. Jodie installed herself next to Jess and selected a history book. Then she got out her rough book and wrote: So who was frolicking yesterday after school with Love God Ben Jones?

Personally I was looking after my granny! Jess wrote furiously in reply.

Whizzer says Ben was late for football because he'd been at your place, wrote Jodie, with a particularly stupid leer.

Holy Moly! It seemed this ridiculous rumour about Ben being at her place was already all over the school. Jess had to see Fred right away and put him straight about it all. He had left his bag by his chair, so maybe he would come back in a minute. The library doors swung open again. Jess's heart leapt. Was it Fred? But no. It was Ben Jones! And he was heading straight for her table! Jodie gave her a knowing wink. Jess froze.

She had been so busy feeling tortured about Fred, she had hardly given Ben Jones a thought since they had parted last night. But here he was now, approaching her table. He was looking particularly gorgeous today. His hair was flicked up in a very cool style and his trainers squelched glamorously. He sat down at Jess's table, looked her straight in the eye and grinned.

Jess was somehow appalled. Normally she would have been thrilled for Ben to sit next to her, but now – what if Fred came back in? If Fred had heard the rumour that Ben Jones had been at Jess's last night, seeing them together now would only confirm it. And Jess knew that when she'd told Fred that lie about being sick, it had really sounded like a lie. Her voice had gone kind of hollow and tinny. Jodie was smirking. Jess was tempted for a moment to seize the nearest heavy dictionary and hit Jodie with it, quite hard.

Jess raised what she hoped was an ironic eyebrow in greeting and returned to her book. She had no idea what her book was about, and since Ben Jones had entered the library she wasn't even sure if it was a book at all. She had to get out of here and away from Ben, or Fred would come back and think the worst.

Ben Jones reached across for the notepad and pen. So this is where you hang out, he wrote. His writing was bizarre: very small and leaning violently sideways, as if a fierce wind had blown on it. Jess's only reply was an enigmatic smile.

Why corals reefs and islands? wrote Ben Jones mysteriously.

Jess frowned. What??!! she wrote.

Your book, he wrote.

Jess looked at her book. It was indeed about coral reefs and islands.

We don't actually read in here, imbecile, she wrote. It's more, like, this is the book I'm wearing today.

I am not an imbecile, wrote Ben Jones. I am aparently a camall.

Dimly Jess remembered comparing various boys to animals. But frankly, who cared? Jess had much more important things on her mind. Although she was still a bit disturbed that Ben could not spell 'apparently', or, more worryingly, 'camel'.

Have you watched the DVD yet? wrote Ben.

Jess made a split-second decision. She would tell Ben about last night – about missing Fred's mum's party. And then she would ask him to clear off so she could sort things out with Fred, on her own.

Come outside for a minute – I need to explain something, she wrote.

They got up and left the table. Ben strolled alongside her. Just as they reached the doors, they burst open and Fred came in. As he saw them facing him, he kind of flinched in a horrible way and raised his eyebrows in a parody of a comedy greeting. Jess looked straight into his eyes, and they flashed like broken glass. He walked past them towards the table where Jess had been sitting. She was sure he'd come back to sort it out with her. But, of course, seeing her going out with Ben Jones put an end to any plan of that sort. Jess had a horrible feeling that the mess she was in was just going to get worse, and worse, and worse.

Chapter 18

Before Jess could say a word to Ben, however, Flora and Mackenzie appeared.

'Serena Jacobs says her uncle's got a garage where we might be able to have band practice,' said Flora. 'We're going there after school to do a recce. Wanna come?'

'Do a recce' was part of Flora's new vocabulary. It came from the world of film. Mackenzie wanted to be a film director. He couldn't just go to the canteen, he had to 'do a recce'. (In other words, have a look around.)

'A garage? Cool!' said Ben, and he turned to Jess. 'You come, too, Jess, yeah?'

'No thanks, I don't trust myself near garages,' she said. 'I'm trying to give them up. Anyway, I can't come – I've got stuff to do.'

Having Flora, Ben and Mackenzie out of the way

would be convenient, in fact. Jess made plans. She would get out of school early and wait for Fred on the wall where he had so often waited for her. And when he appeared, she would pounce and make her apology. It would go like this: 'I shall never ever forgive myself for yesterday, but please say you forgive me, or I might have to go to India and spend the rest of my life cleaning the pavements of Calcutta with my tongue.'

Or how about this: she would fall to her knees at his approach and cry, 'Name an animal – any animal – and I will imitate it in front of the whole school!'

Jess waited on the wall, and Fred did not appear. She waited until all the school buses had gone, packed with cussing and fighting kids. Thank goodness she lived near school and walked home. She felt really sorry for the bus drivers, although she suspected some of the grumpy ones of being Satan's agents on earth. She was glad her dad was not a bus driver, but a glamorous artist in faraway St Ives. By the sea.

She waited until the last few stragglers had dawdled off down the road, fiddling with their mobiles. She began to feel conspicuous. She took out her mobile and sent a text to Flora: HOW'S THE GARAGE? Although really she couldn't care less. But it gave her something to do.

She sent a text message to her dad. ARE YOU BY THE SEA OR WHAT?

Immediately a reply came back: NO I AM IN THE DOCTOR'S WAITING ROOM.

How typical! There he was, living by the sea, and he was wasting this fine afternoon in the doctor's surgery. NOTHING SERIOUS I HOPE?

THERE'S A SPOT ON MY FACE AND I'M JUST CHECKING IT'S NOTHING NASTY.

YOU THINK YOU'VE GOT PROBLEMS! Jess texted back. THERE'S 70 SPOTS ON MY FACE AND THEY'RE ALL NASTY.

There was a pause. Then came the reply: HA HA! IF I DIE OF BLACKHEADS YOU CAN HAVE ALL MY PAINTINGS. DO TRY AND LOOK GRATEFUL! LOVE YOU BEST IN THE WORLD. This was the best moment of the day so far. Text messaging was probably invented for shy dads who could never say 'love you' out loud.

Still no Fred. Where on earth had he got to? Jess had been waiting for nearly an hour. The problem now was how to give up and go home without appearing to have been stood up. It wasn't that there was anyone in particular watching. But Jess was watching herself. You know how it is. So she stared at her mobile, as if waiting for a crucial message which would go: SORRY I CAN'T PICK YOU UP OUTSIDE SCHOOL, DARLING – SEE YOU AT THE RITZ.

Jess was about to get up with the air of one who has just been redirected to the Ritz, when a car pulled out of the school gates, turned left and drove off straight past her. It was the car belonging to the English teacher, Mr Fothergill. Jess recognised it instantly, as it was a yellow sports model. Mr Fothergill, though fat and sweaty in the flesh, was evidently trying for a little extra glamour via his wheels. Jess and Flora called it the 'Greased Banana'.

As the Greased Banana flashed past, Jess suddenly saw Fred sitting in the passenger seat. He did not look at her. His eyes were fixed straight ahead. Was he deliberately ignoring her or just distracted? His profile flashed past, like a head on a coin. Gone. But how mysterious! Why was he in Mr Fothergill's car?

Chapter 19

Jess got home to find Granny installed at the kitchen table. Her mum was not home yet.

'How are you, Granny? Any mass murders in the news today?'

Jess kissed the top of her head. She smelt nicely of lavender talcum powder. Some people's grannies didn't. It was touch and go with old people. They could lose it and start smelling of neglected ponds, just like that.

'There's a mysterious virus sweeping through the hospitals in France,' said Granny. 'And they can't do anything about it. It's the Auntie Biotics,' she warned. 'We're all becoming immune to our own immune systems.'

It seemed that Granny shared the family's rather feeble grasp of the natural sciences. Indeed she might possibly have originated it.

'It starts with vomiting,' said Granny, looking worried. 'Then they can slip into a coma and snuff it within 24 hours!'

'Well, let's be grateful we're not in a hospital in France,' said Jess. 'Do you want some toast, Granny? I'm going to have some. Though you've almost taken away my appetite with all that tasteless talk of vomiting.'

Granny agreed to some toast, and they put the kettle on. Jess was desperate to ring Fred but she had to eat first. If she didn't, her stomach would start this dreadful hollering: '*Worra! Worra! Worraworra! Worraworraworraworra!*' Like distant thunder over the mountains.

Jess banished all thoughts of vomiting by fantasising about the shopping trip to New York. She enjoyed her toast and jam, and then, with a madly beating heart, she rang Fred. The line was engaged. She went back to sit with Granny for another minute.

'I wonder if you'll do a little job for me, Jess,' asked Granny. 'It's fairly disgusting but I'll pay you handsomely.'

'I'd do anything for you, Granny,' lied Jess affectionately. She hoped it didn't involve anything to do with toilets.

'I want you to put my eardrops in,' said Granny.

'Only I'm going to have my ears syringed the day after tomorrow.'

Instantly, Jess was back shopping on Fifth Avenue, stepping out smartly with a couple of Bloomingdale's and Calvin Klein carrier bags. However, she agreed to put Granny's drops in, as soon as she'd made her phone call. Until she'd managed to speak to Fred she was afraid her hands wouldn't stop shaking. And it would be tragic – and possibly fatal – if instead of putting the drops into Granny's ear, they went into her eye, mouth or nose.

She rang Fred again. The number was engaged. Was Mrs Parsons talking to the police?

'My son's description? Oh dear – tall, well, about 5'10" – fair-haired, thin, er, er, strange staring grey eyes. What was he wearing? What was he wearing? Oh heavens, I haven't a clue. Wait! It would have been his grey hood thing and blue jeans. And I know I'm his mother, but although his eyes are grey, sometimes I feel that the blue of his jeans makes his eyes look kind of blue. Please, please, officer, bring back my baby!'

After the fifth attempt to ring Fred, Granny became suspicious. The line was constantly busy.

'Is Flora still on the phone, dear?' she asked.

'It's not Flora, Granny. It's Fred.'

Granny's eyes lit up. 'Aha! A boy! Is it the one who called last night? I thought you looked a bit feverish, love. Is Fred your boyfriend, then?' Granny smiled and winked in a lovable, though slightly obscene manner.

'Certainly not, Granny!' cried Jess. 'He's just a friend. I have no interest in boys, as you know. In my opinion they should all be herded off into wildlife parks. Apart from Flora, Fred is my best mate. I just need to ring him to get some details about homework.'

'Homework?' remarked Granny, looking a little sceptical. 'It all seems a bit desperate for homework.'

Jess felt bad about lying to Granny. She wasn't like Mum. Mum disapproved of almost everything. Boyfriends were going to be the very worst thing of all. Jess actually dreaded having a boyfriend, because of having to tell her mum.

Perhaps she would just avoid it until her mum was 80 or something, and in an old people's home, and then Jess, who would by then be about 50, would drop by and casually remark, 'Oh, by the way, Mum, I've got a boyfriend.' And even then her mum would probably hurtle out of her wheelchair and smack her hard across the face, crying, 'You trash! Get outta my house – I mean, my room!' It was hard, sometimes, being the daughter of a radical feminist who hated men.

'OK, Granny, I admit it – I lied about the home-work,' said Jess. 'It's not about that. It's just a misunderstanding. I really let him down yesterday and he's mad at me. So I just want to apologise.'

Granny nodded and winked, and tapped the side of her nose.

'Why are you winking like that?' demanded Jess. 'Do you know something I don't know?' Or maybe Granny had finally flipped and was sinking rapidly into Alzheimer's, or, as Jess had mistakenly called it when young, Old-Timer's disease.

'Just your best mate, eh?' remarked Granny. 'Ah well – if you say so.' And she got up and shuffled off to the sitting room.

Jess heard the TV being switched on. Granny never missed a news bulletin. There was always something ghastly happening involving body parts.

Jess reached an instant decision. She would run to Fred's house. She would knock at the door. She would apologise there and then – handsomely. If indeed somebody can apologise handsomely when afflicted with seventy spots.

Jess grabbed her jacket, shouted, 'Just going out for half an hour, Granny!' and ran out of the house.

Unfortunately, she met her mum by the gate, and

she could tell by her face that she had had one of those days. Occasionally people came into the library and peed, pooed or got drunk and started shouting abuse. Drunks and vagrants went in to sleep in the Reference section. Once, a very old man who lived on the streets had died on the *Oxford English Dictionary*. You may think that being a librarian would be a quiet, cushy job, but sometimes it seemed that the library was really a nightmarish extension of The Mean Streets and that librarians were just cops and paramedics disguised in tweedy cardigans and long dangly parrot earrings from the charity shop.

'Where do you think you're going?' demanded her mum, in cop mode.

'Just to Fred's – just for a moment – to borrow something.' Jess tried to dodge past her mum, but her arm was seized with frightening strength. She should never have suggested her mum start going to the gym. They struggled briefly by the gate.

'Have you done your homework? Get back indoors!' cried her mum, in a ferocious bad mood even by her standards.

'I'll only be half an hour and I can't do my homework till I've got these notes off Fred!' cried Jess in despair.

Summoning her last shreds of strength, Jess pushed her mum back against the wall, struggled free and ran off. She realised that when she returned she would be in big trouble, but she had to see Fred now. She ran all the way and, when she arrived, rang the bell immediately instead of waiting till she had got her breath back. The door was opened by Fred's dad. Jess could hear football on the TV indoors, and though Fred's dad didn't exactly look furious at her arrival, he was clearly planning to deal with her enquiry with ruthless speed and return to the screen within seconds.

'Is – Fred – in?' panted Jess, hopelessly out of breath. She was going to have to work out, one of these days.

'No,' said his dad. 'Sorry. He's out.'

'Could – you – ask – him – to ring – me, please?'

'OK,' said Fred's dad, obviously hoping that was all.

'Thanks!' gasped Jess, and turned to go.

It was only when she was halfway home that she realised that perhaps Fred's dad had been lying. That Fred was 'out' rather than out. Refusing to see her. On the other hand, he might be halfway to Paris with Mr Fothergill by now. When she was three-quarters of the way home she realised she should have apologised to Fred's dad about not turning up to his wife's birthday party. But she was fairly sure that, given a choice, Fred's dad would rather return immediately to football than endure passionate speeches of guilt and shame.

A hundred metres from home, Jess's mobile bleeped. She grabbed it, hoping it was Fred. But it was only a text message from Flora. **THE GARAGE IS BRILLIANT! RING ME FOR DETAILS!** Jess switched off her mobile, shaking her head in disbelief. As if a mere garage could be of any interest. Flora really should get herself a life.

Chapter 20

Jess's mum was waiting, wrapped in a ferocious glare.

'Sorry!' said Jess. 'But look – I've only been twenty minutes. In fact, eighteen. A mere nothing in evolutionary terms. The blink of an eye.'

'This is my house!' said her mum, spitting fire.

'So?' Jess tried to keep the mood light, playful. She didn't want to tell her mum about how she had ruined Fred's mum's birthday party and was desperate to apologise to the whole Parsons family. It was her major crime in life so far and she knew her mum would be deeply upset to hear about it. 'I love it. It's a great house.'

'Don't you start being cheeky on top of everything else!' hissed her mum. 'This is my house, and I want some consideration from those who live here! After the day I've had, what I want is somebody to make me a cup of tea and tell me they've got an A in English. Instead, I get beaten up on my own doorstep.'

Jess ran to the kettle. It was hot.

'Too late!' said her mum grimly. 'I've made it myself. So where are the precious notes?'

'The precious notes?' repeated Jess, unable to remember for a split second what on earth her mum was talking about. That was the problem with lying. If you lied extensively, as Jess usually did despite constant New Year's Resolutions, you could never remember what it was you were supposed to have done.

'The notes you went to Fred's to borrow.'

'Oh, I couldn't get them. Because he was out. His dad said so.'

'You could have saved a lot of trouble and time by ringing him first.'

'She did ring him first, dear.' Granny was watching from the doorway, evidently hoping this row might develop into a full-scale murder, possibly involving severed body parts. 'She tried several times. She made me some tea and toast as soon as she came in, Madeleine, and we had a lovely chat about her friend Frank.'

'Fred,' corrected Jess. Although she adored Granny, and was deeply grateful for her support right now, if she called Fred 'Frank' again, Jess would scream aloud and might just have to throw custard over her.

'Fred, Fred, Fred, I'm sick of hearing about him!' snapped Jess's mum. 'He rang the other day, and straightaway you were off out to meet him. Haven't you got any dignity? Any pride? Or will you just run off out at the beck and call of any Tom, Dick, or Harry?' Her mum looked cross and ran her fingers through her hair in a tragic and fatigued way.

'What happened then, Mum?' asked Jess, making a huge effort to control her temper. 'Sit down. Let me make you some soup.' Jess pushed her mum down into her chair.

'I'll open a tin of that lovely tomato soup, dear,' said Granny. 'I need a bit of exercise.'

'So what happened in the library?' asked Jess.

'Was anyone taken ill?' asked Granny eagerly. 'I was in the post office once when a man fainted – with a terrible gargling noise. We had to call an ambulance. I never knew what happened to him. It's always worried me rather, but I suppose I'll never know now, because it was in 1974.'

'Oh, nothing happened in the library really,' said Jess's mum. 'Just some teenagers messing around with the computer and being cheeky. Alison didn't come in because she's got flu, so we were short-staffed, and I didn't even get a lunch break. And then a smelly man came in and asked me to explain the system to him. I had to explain it three times and it was only halfway through the third time that I realised he had dementia.'

'Never mind,' said Jess, stroking her mum's hand. 'After supper you can have a lovely bath with lavender oil in it. Or geranium or something.'

'Stop trying to soft-soap me,' said Jess's mum.

'Not soap, mum – bath oil!' Jess grinned.

Granny picked up a saucepan. 'I've managed to get this blasted tin open,' she said in triumph. 'So I can't be completely useless after all.'

Jess's mum crossed her arms on the table, laid her head down on her arms and closed her eyes. 'I'm shattered,' she said.

Granny looked guilty. 'It's all that trouble you had to go to, fetching me over here to live with you.' She shook her head. 'I'm nothing but a nuisance. That great long drive, all the way there, and then the car breaking down on the way back, and having to find us somewhere to stay, and then working flat out to get me settled in and comfy, unpacking all my things. No wonder you're shattered, love. Just take it easy. Jess and I will make the supper, won't we, dear?'

Granny stroked Jess's mum's head in a tender way. It was really odd to think of her being Mum's mum. Once, Jess's mum had been a bald baby, sitting on Granny's knee. The photographic proof was on the dresser. Then Granny had been young and pretty. Family history was such a strange thing. Jess had a photo of her great-grandfather, and he looked just like Freddie Mercury, although he was unlikely to have shared Freddie's exotic lifestyle. Guys didn't go for feather boas and diamanté cat-suits in the north of England in the 1920s.

Freddie . . . Fred. Oh dear! Everything seemed to remind her of him. Jess agreed to help with the supper, even though she hated cooking with a pure, romantic, hot-blooded passion. Maybe she could distract herself with domestic chores. She felt a bit guilty, not just towards Fred, but towards her mum as well. Her mum had done loads of extra work so that she could swap bedrooms with her – moving all her stuff out, moving Jess's stuff in. Her mum's little back bedroom still wasn't sorted. There was a huge pile of black sacks in there. It looked like the doss-hole of a vagrant, not the bedchamber of a distinguished librarian.

The supper was edible – mainly due to Granny's input – and afterwards Jess watched the news without complaining. Her mum still looked tired and rather ratty. Granny was delighted because a mass murderer was on trial in Bosnia. But Jess's mum was plunged back into despair because another war had broken out in Africa.

'I don't know why we watch the news,' she sighed, switching off the TV with unnecessary savagery.

Jess was so tempted to say, 'I told you so. We should have watched MTV,' but heroically remained silent.

'I'm sorry I went out when you told me not to,' she said, now that her mum seemed fairly calm.

Her mum just shook her head in a helpless, hopeless way, as if their little struggle by the gate was a sign of the terrible human tragedy that was life on our planet.

'I just hate the thought of you turning into the sort of little tart who chases boys all the time,' she sighed. 'You were so original and independent as a child.'

Jess stifled the familiar urge to hit her mother quite hard with the nearest heavy object – the urn containing Grandpa's ashes. Granny had placed it on the coffee table earlier so he could enjoy the football. But Jess restrained herself. It was possible that Grandpa had not punished his daughter enough when she was a child. But it would be rather harsh to get a good hiding from your father after he had died.

'I'm still independent,' Jess said in a clenched voice between clenched teeth. 'And I don't chase boys, ever. Fred is not my boyfriend, he never has been, he is just a friend.' Or was.

'I just don't want you to end up heartbroken and discarded,' said her mum. 'It's easily done. Men are such monsters. Most of them.'

'Oh, come off it, Madeleine!' cried Granny. 'Your dad wasn't a monster. He was an angel. Have you forgotten the chocolate drops he used to bring home for you every Friday?'

'No,' sighed Jess's mum. 'I haven't forgotten the chocolate drops.'

'And surely you're not referring to Tim? He's a lovely dad for Jess – isn't he, dear? He was such a polite boy – and he's still a lovely chap. He always remembers my birthday. He sent me a painting of a bunch of flowers last year.'

'Yes, Dad's great,' replied Jess. *It would be quite nice to see him more often, though*, she thought. 'He texts me all the time. He sends me a spoof horrorscope every day. It's cool having a dad who's an artist. Can I go down to Cornwall and stay with him this summer, Mum?'

Jess's mum looked startled and appalled, as if Jess

had suggested spending a few days with Mr Ogre of Ogre Castle.

'Oh, I don't know about that,' she said. 'We wouldn't want to inconvenience him.'

'I am his daughter, Mum, for goodness' sake! And anyway, I've already mentioned it to him,' said Jess. 'When he rang up last time.'

'What did he say?' asked her mum.

'He said he'd see. He didn't rule it out. He seemed quite keen, actually,' said Jess, veering once more towards a convenient untruth.

'I'll have to e-mail him,' said her mum.

Granny smiled eagerly. 'I'm sure he'd love to see Jess this summer, dear. It's so good that you're still on friendly terms, isn't it?'

Jess's mum nodded, and several slightly odd expressions flitted across her face. Jess wondered, for a split second, if her mum was still in love with her dad. Briefly, Jess envisaged a screenplay in which she dragged her mum down to Cornwall and placed her parents together in a magic garden. They emerged ten minutes later, engaged to be, well, remarried. It was a satisfying screenplay, but somehow, in some ultimate sense, kind of boring.

Jess went to bed after that and tried to read Act V of

Twelfth Night. It was homework left over from two days ago. However, Jess was tired, and the lines kept going strangely slanted, a bit like Ben Jones's handwriting. She closed the book and tried to think about Ben Jones for a while. She revisited the screenplay set in Cornwall, dressed Ben in a wetsuit and arranged for him to perform some daredevil award-winning surfing on the beach at St Ives. After the surfing he walked up the beach, fell at her feet and proposed marriage. They were married in Tobago and spent their honeymoon snorkelling and lying under palm trees.

They had just removed their snorkels in order to indulge in a bit of honeymoon snogging, when Jess's mum appeared on the beach. The beach vanished and was replaced by the bedroom, but Jess's mum was still there, kneeling by the bed. She kissed Jess's brow.

'I'm sorry about this evening,' she said. 'Let's see what Daddy says about you going down there. But I'm not sure it's such a good idea.'

'Why not?' said Jess. 'What's the problem?'

Her mum looked furtive, and shrugged.

'Why did you and Dad split up? Do you still love him?'

'Whatever gave you that idea?' exclaimed her mum, in horror. She scrambled hastily to her feet.

'Oh, I just thought it would be cool if you two got

together again. You could renew your vows on a beach somewhere – like Tobago.'

'What an appalling thought,' said her mum, and backed away to the door before Jess could spook her with any more horrific scenarios. 'Not in a million years! Look, Jess. I know I may be a bit prejudiced against men, and I expect it's hard for you, at times, darling, but I can assure you I've got my reasons.'

'Was Dad cruel to you?' called Jess, as her mum opened the door.

'Oh no. Never! Please don't think that. He was fine. It was totally amicable,' said her mum. She went out quickly and shut the door. Jess was puzzled for a while, but there was no point in trying to get to the bottom of her mum's mysteries. However, Jess decided it might be worth pumping Granny for info at the earliest opportunity.

She tried to return to her fantasy about marrying Ben Jones on a Caribbean beach, but something else kept getting in the way. How could she concentrate on fantasies about Ben when her relationship with Fred was so comprehensively trashed?

Suddenly her mum came in. She looked strange. She looked secretive. She looked haunted. She looked mysterious.

'Just one other thing,' she said.

This was it. The moment of truth. The secret behind Jess's parents' marriage. The terrible truth about their doomed love.

'I've just remembered,' said her mum, 'you've got a dentist's appointment in the morning.'

Chapter 21

Jess had no cavities. She silently gave thanks to the Goddess of Teeth: Granny. Jess suddenly remembered, while lying on the dentist's couch, that she hadn't put Granny's eardrops in the night before. She'd have to do it that night.

'I don't want your mother to do it,' Granny had confided darkly. 'Her coordination can be a bit poor when she's tired. I remember once she broke a window trying to bandage my ankle.'

Mid-morning break was just finishing when Jess got to school, so she had to go straight to double maths. Flora was in a different maths set – a higher one, naturally – so Jess wouldn't see her till lunchtime. At lunchtime she went to the library, but Flora wasn't there, and neither, she couldn't help noticing, was Fred. Maybe Flora was in the gym gallery with

Mackenzie and Ben. Jess went there. No sign of them. There was a group of girls with candy-floss hair and candy-floss souls drooling over a boy called Bison doing press-ups.

'Have you seen Flora?' asked Jess, putting on a sour frown of indifference to body-building. She didn't for a moment want to be mistaken for the sort of girl who salivates over a six-pack.

'I saw her and Mackenzie talking to Mr Samuels in the music room,' said one of the girls.

Jess couldn't decide whether to trudge across the whole school to the music department. Why did she have to run around after Flora the whole time? On the other hand, on her way across school she might just run into Fred and be able to apologise to him.

Jess sat down on a low wall by the tennis courts. Some very small kids were trying to play tennis. It was quite amusing, really. A little girl with red hair tried to serve, tossed the ball up and missed it on the way down. It hit her on the nose, and she lost control of her racket, which sailed over the net. This cheered Jess up slightly. She may be tragically alone, abandoned by her best friend and in the middle of a horrid misunderstanding with Fred, but at least she could take pleasure in other people's misfortunes.

Jodie sat down beside her. 'What has Fred asked you to do for his newspaper?' she asked.

Jess blinked in total puzzlement. 'What newspaper?'

'Oh, Jess! Haven't you heard? Mr Fothergill asked Fred to edit a school newspaper and he's been asking everybody to do stuff for it. He rang me last night and asked me to write a piece about the environment. I'd have thought he'd have asked you first.'

A horrid spear of alarm stabbed through Jess's guts. Fred had rung Jodie last night! So he had been home after all! He had been ringing people! But he hadn't rung her – and he'd told his dad to tell her he was out!

'Oh, well, I've been to the dentist,' said Jess. 'I haven't seen him yet.'

'It's brilliant!' said Jodie. 'Fred's even got an office – it says "Editorial" on the door. It's Mr Fothergill's office really, but he's turned it over to Fred just for the rest of the term. We're going to have an editorial meeting in a minute. See you!' Jodie got up and ran off.

Jess turned back to the tennis for teenies. One of them had fallen over and was trying to play while sitting down, and the others were messing about, putting tennis balls inside their shirts and shorts and pretending to be boob queens or well-hung, but somehow it didn't seem so amusing any more.

So Fred had asked Jodie to write a column about the environment. Jodie's idea of a beautiful environment was the shopping mall. And as for writing, well, Jess didn't want to be mean, even privately in her own head, but she didn't think Mr Shakespeare needed to worry about competition from Jodie Gordon.

Maybe if she strolled in a casual kind of way past what used to be Mr Fothergill's office, Fred would be inside – with the door open – and he'd call out, 'Hey! Jess! I've been looking for you all day! I want you to be our comic columnist – right on the front page. Five hundred words about anything you like, and we'll have a photo of you as well, so get your hair cut!'

The hair joke was their best running gag. It was usually Jess who said, 'Get your hair cut!' in a military voice, because Fred's hair was always in his eyes and down over his collar. He could get away with it because he was a famous brainbox – by the standards of Ashcroft School. But Jess had often wondered what Fred would look like with a short cut. Although there was always the risk that he might end up looking like a bushbaby, as he had rather large, saucer-like eyes. *No! That way madness lies*, thought Jess. Comparing boys to animals was a waste of time. Men *were* animals after all.

The door to Mr Fothergill's office was closed, and

there was a notice on it: *Do Not Disturb: Editorial Meeting in Progress*. Jess strode past briskly, as if she hadn't been at all interested in that particular door. She walked on blindly for a minute, not having the faintest idea where she was going, then found herself by the gym again. Oh no! Any minute now she really would be mistaken for a girl who salivates over a six-pack.

She paused, pulled a face to suggest a serious and possibly tragic thought, and looked importantly at her watch. Then she turned on her heel and marched back towards the music room again, as if she had suddenly decided to do something tremendous, such as saving the world single-handed. She had never had such a confusing day. But at least all this exercise might trim her buttocks into shape.

Before she got to the music room, she heard some divine piano playing drifting out on the air. Jess wished she were musically gifted. The nearest she got to playing an instrument was when she flushed the lavatory.

Inside the room were the music teachers Mr Samuels and Ms Dark. Ms Dark was sitting at the piano, and Flora was sitting next to her. Mackenzie was standing behind them, taking a keen interest. Mr Samuels was playing bass, and Ben Jones was sprawling picturesquely on a desk. He looked up as Jess came in and gave her a lovely, lazy, handsome smile.

It was widely rumoured throughout the school that Mr Samuels and Ms Dark were having an extra-marital affair. Mr Samuels was a little overweight but decidedly handsome with black curly hair and a fabulous smile. Ms Dark was fair (life was so contrary), and quite Marilyn Monroe-like from the neck down. They spent lunch hours in their department making beautiful music together and travelled to and from school in Ms Dark's car.

Mr Samuels had a goofy, cross-eyed wife and two cross-eyed, goofy children. Life was indeed contrary. Why hadn't they inherited Mr Samuels' divine looks? Ms Dark, meanwhile, was living with a man who resembled a mass murderer. He had a homicidal nose and a cruel mouth. So while Jess did not approve of teachers having affairs, she thought perhaps in this case it was understandable. If indeed they were having an affair. Somebody said they had seen Ms Dark's car parked after school in Lovers' Lane. But, of course, Ms Dark might just have been walking her dog – a good-looking Schnauzer called Bridlington.

'Jess!' cried Mr Samuels with a delighted smile. 'Just

the very person we need!' He had this way of making you always feel welcome. 'Flora's been telling us about Poisonous Trash – great name, by the way, Flora.'

'Oh – Jess thought of the name!' said Flora, blushing. But would Flora have admitted that if Jess hadn't actually been in the room? Or would she have just taken the credit, smiling her beautiful smile?

'Flora and Mackenzie are just trying to work out a number with Ms Dark,' said Mr Samuels, and he managed to say the name 'Ms Dark' in a caressing kind of way, even though it was such a short, sharp name. Perhaps it was fortunate Ms Dark wasn't called Miss Honeysuckle, or Mr Samuels' spit would certainly have oozed all over the floor tiles. Ms Dark gave Mr Samuels a smile which would have melted the Eiffel Tower, and Mr Samuels gazed in rapture right back at her. Then Ms Dark tore her eyes away from her beloved.

'Maybe you can help us, Jess,' she said. 'We've got in a bit of a tangle with the words.'

'Couldn't Jess join the band?' asked Mr Samuels suddenly. 'You could do with a rhythm section. Drums or something.'

'No!' cried Jess. The man's happiness had clearly turned his head and sent him lurching over the crazy edge of craziness. She wasn't going to be tacked on to

Flora's band as a kind of afterthought! Never, never, never! She was being invited to join in as a patronising sort of kindness. They pitied her tragic, lonely, under-achieving existence. OK, so she wanted, secretly, to be in the band more than anything else on earth. But it was too late now. It was 'their' band. She was an outsider. And she was going to make absolutely sure she stayed an outsider.

'We're going to play in the end-of-term show!' said Flora, her face shining with horrible excitement. 'It's in two weeks, so we're going to have to practise every night after school.'

'Good job the exams are over,' said Mr Samuels, exchanging a secret glance of longing with Ms Dark.

'Great,' Jess said. 'Cool. But I'm afraid I can't make it. I've got, like, so many other commitments.'

'Oh, OK,' nodded Ms Dark. 'You must be helping Fred with the newspaper, right?'

'Well, I won't disturb you any longer,' said Jess, ignoring Ms Dark's inconvenient question. With any luck, by tomorrow she *would* be helping Fred with the newspaper. 'I just wanted to ask Flora if I could borrow her French textbook, cos I've lost mine.'

'Sure,' said Flora. 'It's in my locker. You know the combination.'

'Thanks a lot,' said Jess. 'Have fun!' And she turned to go.

Suddenly Ben Jones slithered down off his desk.

'Yeah, um, I think I'll come, too,' he said. 'Song-writing isn't really . . . my, like, thing.'

He followed Jess out and they walked together towards the courtyard in the middle of the Upper School.

'So. Yeah. Um – where are you going?' asked Ben casually. Jess was too embarrassed to say that she hadn't the remotest idea. So much stuff was whirling around her head that she didn't have a really clear idea of where she was, let alone where she was going next.

'Let's have a drink first, I'm thirsty,' said Jess. They went to the school snackbar and Jess bought them a Coke each and some cheesy biscuits. She insisted it was her turn to treat him, because Ben had paid when they went to the burger bar. Ben was moaning about the band, but Jess found it hard to concentrate.

'OK,' he said eventually, finishing off his Coke. 'Where next? To get the French book from Flora's locker?'

Jess sighed. She now had to go through this charade, even though she hadn't really needed Flora's French book. It had just been an excuse to get away. Every time she told a lie, it kind of recoiled and wound itself around her like a horrible tangle of netting.

'This, like, rehearsing stuff sucks,' said Ben. 'I'm too dumb to write songs.'

Jess tried hard to focus on what he was saying.

'I'm useless at bass guitar, too,' he went on. 'But Mackenzie kind of, like, forced me to. This band is his idea, see?'

'Oh well,' said Jess, politely, 'I'm sure it'll go down a storm. There won't be any other bands playing in the end-of-term show. It'll be just fat girls playing the trumpet.'

'I dunno,' said Ben Jones. 'I think we're gonna be rubbish and make total fools of ourselves.'

'No you won't!' cried Jess. She turned to him with a huge effort, feeling guilty that she hadn't really been concentrating on what he'd been saying for the past half-hour. She made a huge effort and gave him a dazzling, encouraging smile. 'You'll be brilliant, you'll see. And I shall personally organise your fan club.'

They turned a corner and bumped straight into Fred. So the editorial meeting must be over. He blushed. He must have heard Jess's last remark.

'Oh, hi!' he said, trying to look light-hearted and preoccupied.

Jess felt her ribs turn to dust. Here was her chance – and she couldn't say anything, because of Ben being there. Fred looked kind of furtive, and hesitated, as if he needed to say something, even though he looked as if he would much rather be running away.

'Sorry – bit embarrassing,' he muttered.

Jess squirmed. What on earth was coming?

'Could I possibly . . .' Fred stuttered.

Was he going to invite her to write for the newspaper after all?

'Could I possibly, er – have that £20 back?'

Oh no! The money! The money Fred had given her to buy his mum a present! Jess had forgotten all about it!

'Sure, sure, of course – I totally forgot. I've had so much on my mind in the last couple of days – I'm really, really sorry,' she gabbled, rooting around in her bag for her wallet.

She opened her wallet, and then realised she'd used some of Fred's money to buy lunch for Ben just now. Subconsciously she'd noticed that she seemed to be unusually loaded, finance-wise, but it just hadn't sunk in.

'I'm so sorry! I've only got £17.65 right now. I'll pay you back the rest tomorrow.' She handed over the horrible collection of notes and coins to Fred. This was the worst moment of her life so far.

'I can lend you £2.35,' said Ben, and fished the money out of his pocket. 'After all, you did buy me a drink just now.' He gave it to Fred.

Somehow this was even worse. Jess could only pay back Fred with Ben's help. Ben had meant to be helpful and kind, but somehow his very presence was an added torment.

'Thanks, cheers!' said Fred, and backed off. Jess had the terrible feeling that Fred was planning never to speak to her again. He turned his attention to Ben. 'The band . . . Yeah. I'd like you to write something about the band. For the newspaper. A sort of diary about all the rehearsals and everything. All the pre-show nerves, you know, the rehearsals, the rows, that sort of thing.'

'You gotta be joking,' said Ben Jones. 'I can't even write the ABC. Um – hey – Jess could do it, though.'

Fred turned to Jess. A look of frozen politeness filled his eyes. 'I really wanted somebody who was actually in the band to do it,' he said.

'Yeah, sorry,' said Jess. 'I can't. I'm not in the band. Flora will do it. Just ask her.'

'OK, then,' said Fred, with a strange little formal nod. He looked relieved.

'You gotta get Jess to write something, though,' insisted Ben Jones. 'She's, like, a genius with the ole pen, you know.'

Jess wished Ben would shut up. Why, at the very moment when Ben ought to be dignified and silent, did he have this disastrous urge to attempt joined-up speech?

'Sure, sure,' said Fred, sidling past them as if under great pressure of important work. 'Oh yes. I want everybody to write something. Send stuff in, send stuff in.' And he gave a stupid little wave, and hurried away.

The bell rang for afternoon school, which saved Jess from having to make any more polite conversation. Which was just as well, because somehow her insides felt as curdled as if she'd had three milkshakes and an orange. As far as Fred was concerned, she was now just part of 'everybody'. As in 'I want everybody to write something. Send stuff in'. Everybody, even you – what's your name? – ah yes, Jess.

Eventually the meaningless lessons were over, and the meaningless bell rang for end of school, and Jess set off home, trudging through a fog of misery. Poisonous Trash went off to do exciting band practice in Serena's uncle's garage. Fred was snugly tucked up in his editor's office, planning his fascinating newspaper. And Jess was off home to put her fascinating Granny's exciting eardrops in.

Granny did have a surprise for her, however, when Jess arrived.

'A boy rang,' she confided. 'Asking for you. He wouldn't give his name. He said he'd ring again later. I wonder if it was that friend of yours – Fergus?'

Chapter 22

The mysterious boy didn't ring again, though. Jess couldn't risk phoning Fred, in case it hadn't been him. It might have been Ben, or possibly Mackenzie, or even the dreaded Whizzer. After all, he had once squeezed her minestrone. The phone call did give Jess that tiny shred of hope which she needed in order to get through the evening without throwing herself off the kitchen table. Otherwise, putting Granny's eardrops in would have been the highlight of the night.

After supper Jess's mum was watching a programme about the history of England, as she had a crush on Oliver Cromwell. So Jess couldn't distract herself with music channels. She went up to her room and carried on getting her clothes out of plastic sacks and hanging them up. It was a major, major task. It could take years. She might just about have finished it in five years' time. By then it would be time to leave home, and she'd have to start packing it up again.

Who was this boy who had rung and refused to leave his name? Whizzer, who had only been attracted to her because of vegetable soup? Ben Jones, who hung around with her now and then because his best mate was going out with hers? Or Fred, who was hardly on speaking terms with her now, and regarded her as just part of 'everybody'? Heavens! She had been inside that boy's pyjamas. Not at the same time as him, obviously. But it must count for something. Though not, apparently, to Fred.

As Jess walked into school the next day, she bumped into Ben Jones by the noticeboards.

'How did the band practice go?' she asked.

He pulled a face. 'We wuz rubbish,' he said. He didn't say anything about having rung her the night before. So it more or less had to be Fred. But Jess wasn't sure how she was going to find out.

Third lesson was English. Everybody would be there. If Fred had rung her, he might mention it, or give her a sign, or something. If only she had remembered to give him his money back! It had added insult to injury. Poor Fred. He must think she was a monster.

As she entered the English room, Mr Fothergill was

giving out a worksheet. Fred was sitting at the front, reading. He always used to sit at the back with her and Flora. He didn't look up as she came in, or as she passed. She ignored him right back, twice as hard, and sat down with Flora. Mackenzie and Ben Jones were sitting next to Flora. It now seemed impossible ever to see Flora on her own. Jess would have to kidnap her and take her off to a remote mountain hut just to enjoy a girly chat.

Flora gave Jess a dazzling smile, but then turned straight back to Mackenzie and whispered something in his ear. And squeezed his arm.

'Now,' said Mr Fothergill, 'I just want to finish off Shakespeare for this year, so from next lesson we can all concentrate on writing something original. Creative writing. Don't forget, if you want to submit anything for the school newspaper, give it to Fred. How's it going, Fred?'

'Snowed under with stuff,' muttered Fred. 'Can't cope. Contemplating suicide.'

'Good, good,' beamed Mr Fothergill. 'That's the spirit.'

Then Mr Fothergill explained about the final worksheet on *Twelfth Night*. Jess stopped listening. She was thinking about the newspaper. She had so many ideas for it. A Lonely Hearts column, for instance. A gossip column. A cartoon competition. Everyone could do cartoons of the teachers and the winners could be published.

She had so many ideas, but she wasn't going to 'send stuff in'. Fred might not accept it. He might send it back, or just lose it. Why hadn't Fred invited her to write something? He so clearly hated her guts. He had invited Jodie, for goodness' sake, and Jodie could hardly hold a pen.

'OK, get on with it,' said Mr Fothergill.

Jess got on with it. Mr Fothergill had meant the Shakespeare worksheet, but Jess thought she would start with the Lonely Hearts idea.

Girl, 15, charming but insane, 70 spots to support, greasy dark hair, smells slightly of Granny's eardrop fluid, bum looks big in everything, boobs will never win prizes at the village show, crazy moments, imagination tends to run away with her, seeks godlike boy with spiky golden hair that shines like a crown, eyes of swimming-pool blue, and a smile that can make baked beans boil in their can. (Ben Jones, obviously.) No football fanatics, computer geeks or TV violence junkies.

Although, thought Jess, *what sort of boys does that leave?* How limited the male sex was.

Unfortunately, chaps were necessary if you wanted to have a family. If only you could reproduce by pulling a hair out of your head and putting it in water. Pretty soon it would sprout roots, like Mum's geranium cuttings, then you would pot it up and put it on a sunny windowsill. A huge bud would form. You'd have to support it in a kind of net, like melons in greenhouses. Then, one day, you would hear a lusty cry. You'd rush to your windowsill and find the bud had burst open and a bouncing baby had dropped off into the net. Then all you had to do was think of a name for it.

Jess was into names of places at the moment. India was a nice name for a girl. Wyoming. San Francisco – although San Francisco sounded like a person's name already. Jess realised it was probably Spanish for St Francis. She remembered St Francis was the saint who loved the birds. Eagle would be a good name for a boy. Albatross. Not Raven, though – the child would inevitably get called a Raven Lunatic.

The bell rang for the end of the lesson.

'Jess!' called Mr Fothergill. 'Can I see how you're getting on, please?'

Horror seized Jess. It was too late. She hadn't done a single answer on the worksheet. She had had no idea that sixty minutes had passed. It felt like about five. The rest of the class went off. Flora pulled a sympathetic face and slipped Jess half a bar of chocolate. Flora, of course, had been writing away at about seventy miles an hour and had completed the worksheet exactly on time.

Fred stayed behind to ask Mr Fothergill something. Jess made an 'after you' kind of gesture to suggest he should go first. She didn't want Fred to see her being humiliated by Mr Fothergill. Fred nodded a horrid polite 'thank you' and dived in.

'It's about the football reports,' he said.

Jess immediately stopped listening. Instead she looked at the back of Fred's head. His hair was practically down on his shoulders. It looked awful. If only he would get it cut.

Eventually Fred and Mr Fothergill sorted out the thing about the football reports, and Fred left the room without a backward glance. Jess shrugged and placed her pieces of paper on the table.

'What is this?' asked Mr Fothergill, peering at Jess's sketches.

'I got bored,' said Jess. 'So I invented a third sex.'

'What about Shakespeare?' asked Mr Fothergill.

'I was going to start the worksheet in a minute,' explained Jess. 'But suddenly the bell went. I'm really sorry. I lost all track of time.'

Mr Fothergill should have been cross, but instead he went on looking at what Jess had done.

'I like this Lonely Hearts ad,' he said. 'Listen, Jess – you should be doing something for the newspaper. A spoof Lonely Hearts column is a great idea. I'll tell Fred you're going to do it, OK?'

'I'm sorry,' said Jess, 'but I don't really want to write for the newspaper.'

Mr Fothergill frowned. His pudgy cheeks sort of drooped. He looked like a disappointed pig. Jess didn't want to hurt his feelings.

'It's a great idea, the newspaper, I love it, and I can't wait to read it,' she added hastily. 'I just can't, like, take part right now. Sorry.'

'Why not?' asked Mr Fothergill.

Jess hesitated. If Mr Fothergill had been a woman teacher, Jess wouldn't have hesitated for a moment. But she wasn't used to talking to men about emotions and stuff. In her limited experience, they usually went pale and ran off to watch football on TV with the sound turned up very loud.

'It's bad vibes,' she said. 'Between Fred and me.'

Mr Fothergill hesitated, and pulled a face. You could see he was longing to escape into football, but there was none available in the classroom.

'OK, well, I won't force you,' he said sort of shiftily. 'But what about the end-of-term show? You did tell me once you wanted to be a stand-up comedian. The show would probably be a better idea for you anyway. You could do a monologue about a girl trying to draft a Lonely Hearts advert. Use this as a starting-off point. OK?'

Jess was suddenly terrified, and yet thrilled. She could be in the show! Not as part of Poisonous Trash, but up there on stage in her own right. Doing stand-up. She was so excited, she almost couldn't speak. So she nodded.

'Great!' said Mr Fothergill. 'I'll tell Mr Samuels and Ms Dark – they're organising it. Once you've got a draft of your monologue, I'd be happy to go through it with you, and we should rehearse it in the school hall, so you're used to the acoustics. So let me know as soon as you've got it ready. And we've only got a few days, so get a move on.'

'What . . .' Jess hesitated. 'What about the Shakespeare worksheet?'

'Oh, heavens, yes!' said Mr Fothergill. 'Let me have it by tomorrow morning, or there'll be big trouble. Well . . . medium-sized trouble, anyway,' he concluded, with a plump piggy grin. Mr Fothergill was really nice. Jess would never eat bacon again.

It was lunchtime. Flora and the guys had gone off to a small practice room to work on their songs. Mr Samuels and Ms Dark had said they could use it in the lunch hour. There was only a piano in there, but Flora was having piano lessons (naturally, Grade 5) so she could play a bit, and Mackenzie had brought his guitar. The music teachers would be very busy from now until the show, practising with choirs and instrumental groups, and possibly also sneaking off to Lovers' Lane now and then, but Poisonous Trash didn't need any more help. They could practise by themselves. Mackenzie had said so. He was full of confidence. They didn't need anybody, he said. And they certainly didn't need Jess.

She didn't care, though. Now she'd got a project of her own. But first she must have food. Fuel for the brain. She was starving, so she bolted down a chicken salad baguette in the canteen. She sat on her own. She didn't want chat. Her mind was racing.

Five minutes later, her lunch was finished. Jess went to the library and sat at a table by herself. She got out a piece of paper and her pen. Right. She'd got to write a monologue that would would have them rolling in the aisles. She'd show Flora how brilliant she could be. She'd show Fred! This was her big chance. She was going to do stand-up. Big Time.

Chapter 23

For a few days, Jess's routine was the same: in every moment of her spare time, she was in the library, working on her monologue. It was the one thing that offered an escape from the black cloud that was her problem with Fred. When Jess was concentrating on her monologue, she forgot about everything else. 'I'm trying to draft this Lonely Hearts ad but instead I'm slowly losing the will to live . . .'

All morning she was looking forward to getting back to it at lunchtime. '*Young female flat-chested ape with bum so huge it blots out the sun . . .*' All afternoon she was looking forward to getting back to it after school. '*Goddess, 15* . . . Or maybe that should be *Minor Deity* . . . Well, to be honest, *Minor Deity with a colourful range of skin ailments* . . .' She got a peculiar excited feeling whenever she thought of it – similar to the feeling she used to get in the days when she worshipped Ben Jones from afar. She was even more crazy about her monologue than she had been about Ben.

She hadn't exactly stopped being crazy about him. Not altogether. But it had changed. He often chatted to her. But whenever she was with him, she seemed kind of the opposite of excited. He was so laid back. Ben's blue eyes and lazy grin were still a great sight in the mornings, but then what? Ben seemed more interested in talking about Flora and Mackenzie than in mapping out a future in which he and Jess were going to enjoy snorkelling and snogging on a Caribbean beach.

Ben found her sitting on a bench by the sports field one morning at break. 'Yeah – er, Flora and Mackenzie are having a row,' he said. 'So I cleared off.'

'A row?' asked Jess. 'What about?'

'Oh, loads of things,' said Ben with a shrug. 'They're always on at each other in band practice.'

'Really?' Jess found this interesting, though not as interesting as her monologue, which she had been thinking about when Ben arrived. 'Aren't they getting on, then?'

Ben sighed and shrugged. 'You tell me,' he said. Then he turned his face to the sun and closed his eyes.

'What are they rowing about?' asked Jess.

'Oh, it's the band,' said Ben. 'Mackenzie says, er, because the band was, like, his idea, he's got to have the final word on everything, yeah? But Flora's not the kind of girl you can just, like, dominate. You know – she's intelligent 'n' stuff.'

Jess did not know whether to be pleased that Ben was praising her friend, or jealous. She decided on jealousy because it was more interesting.

'Unlike me,' she observed with an ironic laugh.

'You?' Ben turned back to her, open-eyed with astonishment. 'You gotta be kidding. You're, like, light years more intelligent than any of us.'

Wow! This was almost enough to make Jess fall for Ben all over again. However, even though he may have thought she was super-intelligent, somehow he still didn't hold her hand, or play with her hair, or stare into her eyes or any of that stuff that Mackenzie did with Flora.

'Flora,' he continued, staring into the middle distance, 'wants to do it, like, her way. She wants to play keyboards and sing from there. Mr Samuels says he can fix up the mikes that way, no problem. But Mac thinks she should be, er, well, standing up and dancing, you know – like, well, doing the whole pop video thing.'

'I see,' said Jess. 'What do you think?'

'Um – I guess I'm on Flora's side,' said Ben. 'She doesn't have to, like, prance about wearing a short skirt. It's – well, tacky. I prefer the idea of her, you know, like, at the keyboards. It looks more, um – classy.'

Although he looked like an angel newly dropped from above, Ben Jones did seem to talk good sense. Even if the words came out rather slowly.

'But, well, um – there's a worse problem even than that, yeah?' he said. 'Basically we're *bad*. We're gonna look rubbish. The band sucks. In fact – um, er, well, will you do something for us, Jess?'

A spear of fear went through Jess's heart. Not, please not join the band! No, no, no – not now she'd got her monologue coming along so well. Not now the band seemed torn with arguments and possibly also sucked. But would she have the guts to say no to Ben Jones, if that was what he asked?

'Could you, like, come and watch us rehearse tonight? Maybe come up with some, um, ideas how we can get it together?' said Ben. 'Otherwise, we're, like, doomed.'

'Of course!' said Jess. 'But tomorrow, not today, yeah? I need to talk to Flora about it first. Make sure she's cool about it.'

'OK,' said Ben Jones. 'And when you've seen what we're like, don't be, like, polite. Tell us like it is, OK? Give it to us straight.'

'Sure,' said Jess.

Ben got up off the bench.

'Thanks,' he said, and reached down and patted her shoulder. 'You're, um, immense. Gotta go now – football practice.'

And he strolled off. The place where his hand had been sort of glowed. This was the first time Ben Jones had ever touched her. If Ben Jones had touched her shoulder a few weeks ago, she wouldn't have washed for a month. Possibly even a year.

Her shoulder would have become a Holy Relic, preserved in a glass case and dressed with fresh flowers each day. She could have made a fortune offering it to girls to kiss. She would have made a sign, saying: *Ben Jones touched my shoulder – see the miraculous imprint of his fingers – or pay a small charge up front to kiss the place brushed by the palm of his hand.* But now it had happened, Jess couldn't help feeling he had patted her in the way he might have shown his affection for a faithful old dog. And rather a smelly one, at that.

The way he talked about Flora, on the other hand, suggested something else. Ben was always talking about Flora. The very first time he and Jess had had coffee together, he'd asked about her. Probably the whole time he'd been with Jess, apparently just chatting casually about this and that, he'd been secretly trying to get the conversation around to the subject of Flora, to find out more about her. Perhaps just to hear the divine music of her name. Ben had got the hots for Flora! The name of a goddess. Jess's only comfort was that it was also the brand name of a margarine.

Man, did she feel sick! Maybe she had still cherished some hopes of a relationship with Ben Jones. But she had been so preoccupied recently. There had been the trouble with Fred (who hadn't spoken to her for ages), the struggle to write a comic monologue and the huge task of catching up with all the schoolwork she had somehow failed to hand in. And in her spare moments she had wondered why her parents had split up. There hadn't really been much time to focus on Ben Jones.

OK, he had often chatted to her. But it had never been anything remotely like being chatted *up*. Jess had got used to the way things were with Ben. But she had been sort of hoping that he was just a slow starter. That after, say, six months of talking about the band, and football, and Flora, and Mackenzie, he would put his arm round her and say, 'You really look fantastic today.' And then – a girl can dream – actually kiss her or something. Before she went senile and died of extreme old age.

But this was never going to happen now, because all the time he'd never really been interested in her. Only in Flora. Jess felt so extremely sick, she had to take an instant mental trip to New York, where she admired all the beautiful glass and enamel in Tiffany's and finally bought an exquisite table lamp for $50,000. And even then she still felt faintly nauseous for the rest of the day.

That evening she phoned Flora. She guessed she would be back from band practice by now.

'Oh Jess!!' cried Flora. She who is adored by millions. 'I've had such a bum day. Mackenzie is really getting up my nose. He wants me to sing standing up and prancing about like a tart, but I want to do keyboards. B.J. says he thinks it'd be a good idea if you looked in on one of our rehearsals and gave us some advice. He really, like, respects your judgement, and so do I. So we insisted and Mackenzie had to back down. Please say you'll come and listen to us tomorrow night after school. Oh please! Only you can save us from TOTAL HUMILIATION!'

Jess was tempted by the thought of them writhing in

total humiliation. A part of her wanted to be there in the front row, enjoying the spectacle. But she couldn't, in all conscience, let her oldest friend down. It wasn't Flora's fault she was irresistible, exquisite, the Queen of Hearts. They had had quite a few laughs over the years. Jess felt she must be loyal to Flora, come what may. And she didn't like the thought of Ben Jones being made to look an idiot, either. Even if he did love Flora instead of her. Heck, who didn't?

'OK,' said Jess. 'I'll come.'

'And maybe after you've told us how we can improve our performance, you could do your monologue for us,' suggested Flora. 'And we could, like, tell you how to improve it.'

It was a good job they were talking on the phone, not person to person. Or at this point Jess would have killed Flora deftly with a small piece of paper, an empty yoghurt pot – anything handy.

'Maybe,' replied Jess. But secretly she thought, *I would sooner see my mum dancing naked in front of the school than let Flora and Co. hear a single word of my monologue, or presume to tell me how to improve it.*

She sighed. That was one of Fred's favourite phrases: *I would rather my mum danced naked* . . . He certainly had a way with words. But as he hadn't addressed a single word to her for such a long time, Jess had to assume they were now mortal enemies. Her terrible revenge would be to make him laugh so much at her monologue that he would wet his pants. Her monologue was Jess's secret weapon. With it she was going to blow them all away.

Chapter 24

Serena's uncle's garage was way out on the edge of the city, surrounded by building sites and the station car park, so it was a good place to practise: no neighbours to complain about the noise. Serena's uncle was divorced and worked long hours as a truck driver, so the band virtually had the place to themselves. And because he was a truck driver, the garage was enormous – it wasn't a one-car garage, or a two-car garage, but a three-truck garage. In fact, there was a big truck parked in there, awaiting repairs, and still a huge amount of space for the band to perform.

Jess waited for them to get ready. Mac and Ben were tuning their guitars and fiddling with amps; Flora was getting changed into her performance outfit. Because, of course, clothes advice was just as important. Even Mac had climbed into his Gothic gear for the occasion. While she waited, Jess got her notebook out and jotted down a couple of ideas for her monologue.

Why do people in Lonely Hearts Ads describe themselves as 'attractive'? If they're so incredibly attractive, why are they advertising in Lonely Hearts anyway? And if male heart throbs are supposed to be tall, dark and handsome, why do I fantasise about a life of lethargy and flatulence with Homer Simpson?

'OK, I'm ready!'

Flora appeared. Jess looked up, and her eyeballs nearly fell out. Flora, who normally looked so classy, had got herself up like a trashy drag queen. She was wearing leopard-skin high-heel boots, leather mini, basque, cleavage, suspenders, a spiky Gothic neck-lace, hair sticking out all over, black lipstick in a massive pout and purple eyeshadow that made her look as if she'd gone twelve rounds with a pack of Rottweilers. It seemed that Flora had abandoned the idea of being on keyboards and had reconciled herself to fronting the band.

'It's trash-cart chic,' she announced.

'Amazing!' said Jess, choking back a giggle.

'OK!' said Mackenzie. 'Let's get on with it.'

Ben Jones picked out a few random notes on his bass guitar, then they all took up their positions, Mackenzie tweaked the synthesiser, and a terrible deafening noise broke out. Jess, though used to loud noises, couldn't help flinching as if an express train had thundered past three inches from her face. Flora abandoned her usual grace and composure, crouched like a baboon and began to scream. Though what exactly she was screaming was a mystery.

'*I got da aaaaarnkh! I faaaaaarchla plaaaaaanch! I wanna grukkkkka plukkka faaaaaaachnyna raaaaaaaaaaaatch!*'

Then she started jumping up and down, while somehow still crouching, and shaking her head violently from side to side. There was a strange expression on her face. She was sticking out her top teeth and squinting her eyes. Then she swept an imaginary audience with a pop-eyed gaze, stuck out her tongue and waggled it violently.

'*I wanna laaaaaaaaarnch!*' (What was that? She wanted lunch?) '*I shaaaaaakkkka kraaaaaaanch! I smaaaaaashshshsha carrannna smakkka flaaaaggggga straaaaaaanch!*'

Jess was filled with a desperate, desperate, desperate

desire to laugh. She mustn't. She mustn't. She looked away from Flora, hoping to fight off this demented giggle by watching Mackenzie instead. But he was doing something completely stupid with his guitar, kind of fighting with it. Only Ben Jones managed to retain some kind of dignity, plucking away at the bass line, but now Jess had got used to the sheer noise, she realised that many of his notes were just plain wrong.

Suddenly it stopped. They all stared at her, panting.

'Amazing!' stammered Jess. It was a useful word, doing great service today. For once, Jess could think of nothing more to say.

'We've got another number, too,' said Mac. 'A quieter one. Let's go!'

Jess hoped that during this quieter number she would stop wanting to laugh. She must not, must not, must not, must not laugh. The quiet number was even worse, though. At least during the noisy number Flora had been screaming. Now she was singing. And – oh my goodness! It was horribly obvious that she was tone deaf.

Mind you, she wasn't getting much help from Mackenzie and Ben. Their random twangings sounded like a gang of bears who had broken into a tool shed.

'*At naiaiaiaiaight . . . Iyn mah beyyyyyyyd . . . Ah finkofyew!*' hooted Flora, with all the soaring beauty of a vacuum cleaner desperately in need of a service. '*When vah moooooon . . . Iys reyd . . . Ah finkofyew!*'

Jess had stopped breathing. It was like being forced to watch a car crash in slow motion. The desire to laugh, instead of going away, was growing bigger and bigger like a high-speed pregnancy. It had filled her ribs and was crawling relentlessly up her throat.

'*Wow wow, whoa oooh!*' wailed Flora suddenly, shaking her head in tragic despair. Jess was reminded of a small dog she had once taken for walks. He used to bark just like that. '*Whaaaaaa . . . Oh whaaaaaaaaa . . . Didyew treeeetme laaaaaaaike . . . A fule . . .*'

Jess had to laugh. She just had to. Her only hope was to disguise it as a coughing fit. She grabbed her bag and whipped her hankie out. Thank goodness her mum had insisted, all these years, on her taking a handkerchief everywhere. Give the woman a medal!

Jess delivered the first few salvoes of laughing into the hankie while the band was finishing their number and, when the music suddenly stopped, she stood up, covering her face and coughing fit to bust.

'S'cuse me – bit of asthma – got to get some fresh air – do that number again – I'll be back in a minute,' she choked, and staggered out.

She walked across the empty car park, hiding her face in the hankie and coughing theatrically, until she heard the band start into the number again.

'*At naiaiaiaiaight . . . Iyn mah beyyyyyyyd . . . Ah finkofyew!*'

Flora's singing was a revelation. To think that such a terrible noise could come out of such a beautiful face! It set Jess off again. She found a corner of the car park where there was a low wall, sat down and howled with laughter until she wept. She laughed until she whimpered. She laughed until she was sure that there wasn't a single scrap of laughing left inside her. She felt quite empty and shaken, and had to brush away tears before she walked back to the garage, as carefully as possible, as if her body were held together with frail thread. She entered the garage just as the number ended.

They all looked at her with a mixture of hope, defeat and frustration. Flora looked hopeful. Ben looked defeated. Mackenzie looked frustrated. Suddenly Jess felt very sorry for them. Poor fools. In five days' time they were going to be on stage in front of the whole school. They shifted uneasily, all staring at her in an imploring way. Ben Jones caught her eye.

'Go on, admit it, yeah?' he said, trying for a little joke. 'We are, like, so bad.'

Mackenzie looked furious. Flora looked insulted, but desperate.

Jess hesitated. If she just praised them and tried to boost their confidence, she would be standing back and doing nothing: delivering them without any warning to the ridicule of the whole school. But how on earth could they get better enough to perform in only five days? Flora would never be able to sing if she practised for twenty years. Jess uttered a silent prayer to the Goddesses of Rock Music. *Please*, she implored, *show me the way out of this*.

Then a miracle happened. Her mouth opened, and these words came out: 'No, no, you're fine. I think the problem is you're not nearly bad enough. I just had this thought while I was dealing with my asthma, you know, why not *deliberately* be as bad as you possibly can? In fact, instead of being yourselves, why don't you, like, invent three personas – you know, real, like, losers or airheads or idiots – and rewrite the songs so they're really really terrible. I think it could really, like, work, as sort of comedy-rock, if you get me?'

A wonderful thing happened. Relief, excitement and gratitude broke out across their faces.

'Brilliant!' cried Mackenzie. 'Then it doesn't matter if we play a wrong note – because we'd be the idiots doing it, not us!'

'And it wouldn't matter if I sing badly!' said Flora. 'Oh Jess! You're a genius!' And she ran up to Jess and gave her a huge hug, which hurt quite a lot because of the Gothic necklace.

Ben Jones just said, 'Great! Great!' sort of quietly to himself.

'You could even say a few words each before you started.' Jess was warming to the idea now. 'Sort of introducing yourselves, you know – so everybody knows it's not meant to be you. You could be, like, "Hi. I'm Aaron Prendergast and this is my band Elastic Poodles. Let me introduce Jules Nerdstone on bass and our lead singer Jolene Brassiere . . ." You could each say something really nerdy and, like, corny, then do the song – as badly as possible.'

'Write it down! Write it down!' shrieked Flora. 'What you said just then!'

'Yeah, you should write our lines,' said Ben. 'You'd be brilliant. You've, like, saved our lives, yeah?'

Jess smiled and shrugged modestly. It was a slight

exaggeration to say she'd saved their lives. But it was nice to feel useful. Ben gave Jess a look that shone with love of the purest, purest sort. Too bad it was the purest sort, thought Jess. But at least it was a start.

Chapter 25

The next few days were hectic. The band got their act together. Jess sat in on another practice. Now that they were trying to be funny, they were not so funny, of course. This time, Jess had to pretend to laugh, whereas the previous time she'd had to pretend she wasn't laughing. Comedy is so complicated.

However, the band's act now looked OK. Jess had made sure they wouldn't disgrace themselves. She had also given Flora some slightly treacherous advice.

'You could make Jolene a bit more outrageous in her, like, dress and make-up,' advised Jess. 'I mean, really really repellent.' She was looking forward to that fair sight.

Mr Fothergill had offered to help Jess practise her stand-up routine, so they went to the English Department after school, two days before the show.

Trembling slightly, and with her heart thudding like a disco backing track, Jess plunged into her routine.

'*Girl, 15* . . . wait a minute . . . *Girl*? Hmmm. How about *Chick*? . . . *Bird*? . . . *Female*? Argh! I'm trying to draft this Lonely Hearts ad but I'm slowly losing the will to live. I can't even get the first word right –' Jess was distracted for a moment by a kid who knocked on the door.

'Go away!' yelled Mr Fothergill. This wasn't a very good start. 'Sorry, Jess,' he said. 'Carry on!'

'Shall I start again?' asked Jess.

'No, it's OK – carry on from where you were!' Maybe he just wanted it to be over, fast. Jess cringed, but forced herself to go on.

'*Girl, 15. Girl.* Ugh! I so hate the way *Girl* is so . . . girly. It sounds so naive and helpless. I can just see her weeping over an injured robin or embroidering rosebuds on an oven glove. *Gothwitch*? OK. *Gothwitch, 15, with bum like mountain range* . . . no, it just doesn't equate. How about *Demon Goddess*? . . . *Part-time minor deity with slight touch of acne*? Hmmm. Perhaps *Girl* is safer ground after all.'

Mr Fothergill smiled in a rather encouraging kind of way. But was he only being polite? Jess gritted her teeth and continued.

'OK, so we have *Girl, 15* – well, can't do much about that unless I lie about my age. And it didn't work when I tried to rent that adult-rated movie. *Girl 15* . . . *attractive? Not unattractive?* Still not strictly true, but those poor fools will be none the wiser. Hmmm. Has anybody ever said anything complimentary about me? Uhh . . . well, when I was a baby, my granny did once say I was charming. Although moments later she was just as enchanted by a passing mongrel with fleas. OK, so we ditch the *attractive*.

'*Girl, 15, house-trained*? Well, it's something, though, isn't it? And call me old-fashioned, but it's a quality one would look for in a girlfriend.'

Mr Fothergill laughed – a little growl of a laugh, like a small dog who is hoping for a biscuit.

'*Charming* is a good concept, though. You can look like the rear end of a dinosaur and still aspire to be charming. And I do. OK: *Girl, 15, charming but – let's face it – insane; likes: vampires, Siberian tigers, friendly nuns and little else. Hobbies: burping for England – in fact, flatulence in general (all mine is of Olympic standard), tending to my granny's ears (oh yes, I have what you might call a lifestyle) and* . . . what else? What are my other leisure pursuits? *Sitting down, occasionally interrupted by short but delightful periods of standing*.'

Mr Fothergill laughed again – out loud! *I love him! I love him!* thought Jess. Not in a gross pervy way – she would have loved anybody who laughed at one of her gags. Mr Fothergill laughed big and long. His laugh was a bit like Santa Claus's: 'HO HO HO!' It was kind of weird, but Jess was immensely grateful, and ploughed on with more confidence to the end.

'Great! Excellent!' he said. 'Well done! I'll make a photocopy of your script, if I may – since you've memorised it now. Then I can prompt you if you forget your lines during the performance. Just one thing – I think you should be sitting at a desk. I know it's called "stand up" but this time it can be "sit down". Then you can actually be scribbling things on a piece of paper as you try to draft your ad, and every time you screw up a piece of paper and chuck it away, you can throw it into the audience. They'll like that.' Mr Fothergill was wasted at Ashcroft School. He should be directing in Hollywood.

'I'll take you home now,' he said, once Jess had tried out the routine sitting down, and he had photocopied the script.

'Oh, it's fine, I can walk, it's not far,' said Jess.

'No, I'll drop you off at home,' said Mr Fothergill, 'in case your mother's worried.'

'My mother only worries about the International Situation,' said Jess.

'In that case,' said Mr Fothergill, 'she must be out of her mind with terror.'

He picked up his jacket and switched out the lights. They strolled down the corridor.

'We've just got to pick up Fred,' said Mr Fothergill.

Jess's heart lurched. She and Fred had not exchanged a word or a look, let alone an ape impersonation, for ages. Suddenly her legs felt as if they were made of cooked spaghetti. They reached the door of the Editorial Office. It was open. Fred was inside, tapping away frenziedly at his PC keyboard amid a chaos of papers.

'Home time, Fred,' said Mr Fothergill.

Fred looked up, saw Jess and suddenly went pale. And then he went red.

'How's it going?' asked Jess politely.

'Fine, thanks,' said Fred. He shut down the computer, got up and stuffed a few pieces of paper in his bag. He didn't look at her.

'Fred's looking forward to acting as theatre critic for the show,' said Mr Fothergill. Jess felt sick with fear. 'He says he's going to rip everyone to shreds.'

'When does the newspaper come out?' asked Jess, too paralysed with horror to say anything interesting.

'The beginning of next week,' said Mr Fothergill, as they walked across the car park towards the Greased Banana. 'I'm afraid my car is a sporty two-seater, but I'm sure you two can squash up together, just for a half-mile or so.' Mr Fothergill unlocked the car with the carefree, cheery manner of a practised torturer. 'You get in first, Fred. Jess won't mind sitting on your knee, will you, Jess?'

'Oh no,' said Jess. 'It'll be good practice for when I sit on the knee of the editor of *The New York Times*.'

'You'll probably *be* the editor of *The New York Times*, Jess,' said Mr Fothergill, opening the passenger door.

Fred clambered in clumsily, and Jess, urged on by Mr Fothergill, fell in on top of him.

'Sorry,' said Mr Fothergill, 'but I'll just have to fasten the seat belt. It'll go round both of you, no problem.'

Fastened together in hostile misery, Jess and Fred waited while Mr Fothergill got into the driver's seat, messed around with his glasses, dropped his keys and generally wasted time. Eventually the Greased Banana started with a roar. Jess could feel the warmth of Fred's lap. He was sitting very still, and was totally silent – no doubt in deep shock. Jess felt hot. She felt cold. She shivered. Mr Fothergill drove out along the road, merrily chatting about theatre critics. Jess and Fred were both speechless at the ghastliness of their situation. It was Mr Fothergill's turn for a monologue now, but he didn't seem to notice.

Eventually they got to Jess's house, and she climbed out.

'Thanks for the lift, Mr Fothergill,' she said. 'Sorry I was so heavy, Fred,' she added clumsily, not looking him in the eye. 'Gotta lose some weight. Bye!'

The Greased Banana roared off again. Jess walked up her garden path, relieved and yet somehow a bit sorry that this bizarre episode was over. It was the first time she had ever sat on a boy's lap.

How ironical that it should have been Fred's. He must have hated every minute. She had felt hot and cold and shivery with a mixture of excitement and horror. If it was like that with a boy she hated, what would it be like with Ben Jones? Although she wasn't sure she and Ben would ever get on lap-sitting terms. Jess thought it was more likely that she might one day sit on a red-hot barbecue, or a live alligator.

'Hello, love!' cried Granny perkily. 'There's been a massacre in Venezuela!' Always so cheerful in the face of disaster. 'And I've made a coconut cake!'

Halfway through the coconut cake, Jess noticed that

she had a bit of a sore throat. Later, watching *Jurassic Park* with Granny, Jess had another attack of shivering. She felt hot. She felt cold. Maybe it hadn't been the horror of sitting on Fred's lap. Maybe it was the flu.

'You look a bit flushed, love,' said Granny. By the time her mum came in from her peace meeting, Jess was lying on the sofa covered up with Great Grandpa's army blanket. Her mum took her temperature. It was 39 degrees.

'That's two degrees of fever,' she said. 'You must go to bed. Oh my goodness! My baby! I was out at a stupid meeting and all the time you were ill!' Whenever Jess was ill, her mum came over all sentimental and slushy. 'Darling! I'll get you some scrambled egg!'

'I don't want scrambled egg!' croaked Jess. 'I don't like scrambled egg even when I'm well!'

'Yes, of course, sorry, I'm such an idiot!' said her mum, helping Jess upstairs and fussing around, making the bed ready. 'Oh no! We've run out of Vitamin C!'

'What's her temperature in Fahrenheit?' shouted Granny from the bottom of the stairs.

'About a hundred, I suppose,' replied her mum.

Jess didn't like the sound of that. A hundred! It sounded terrible. What if she died? Well, if she did, at least Fred would be sorry.

Jess ran a little video in her head in which Fred came to her funeral, inconsolable with grief, and visited her grave every day for the rest of his life, sobbing and chucking rosebuds about. Also, because she had sat on his lap, he never washed his knees again. Although probably he never washed them anyway.

All night she shivered and shook. Every bone in her body ached. She couldn't move. Peculiar feverish dreams came and went. She was riding on the wing of an aeroplane. The traffic in town was being directed by a gigantic naked baby. Worst of all, she was doing her stand-up routine and she couldn't remember the words. When she woke up next day, her sheets were wet with sweat.

'My poor baby! You can't possibly go to school today,' said her mum, mopping her brow with a horrible smelly face flannel.

Jess knew she couldn't go to school. It was enough of a challenge just to walk the few steps along to the bathroom.

'It's the flu,' her mum said. 'You'll probably feel better by the weekend.'

'But it's the show tomorrow,' croaked Jess. 'I've just got to get better for that.'

'I'm sorry, love,' said her mum. 'But I think you'd better put that right out of your mind.'

231

A huge, bitter disappointment engulfed Jess. The one day of the year when she was really longing to go to school – the one day when she might have something really special to offer – was tomorrow. And it was just not going to be possible. Her body had let her down. Silently Jess cursed the God of Influenza. She bit her lip hard, trying not to cry, but she did snivel a bit into her pillow after her mum had gone downstairs. In fact, the flu had made her feel so weak, she broke down in tears every time she thought of the TV adverts for the animal shelter.

Desperately, Jess tried to think of a bitter joke to cheer herself up, to keep the tears at bay. Eventually she thought of one. At least her performance wouldn't be ripped to shreds by Fred in his role as theatre critic.

Chapter 26

The next day Jess was still ill, but she managed to go downstairs. Her mum made up a bed for her on the sofa. Granny could take care of Jess while her mum was at work, as long as she didn't have to go up and down stairs.

Jess's mobile phone began to beep. Her dad had heard she was ill and started to text her.

WHAT SORT OF FLU IS IT? he said. WHAT IS YOUR TEMPERA-TURE? TELL GRANNY TO GIVE YOU LOTS OF DRINKS.

MY TEMP IS 203, replied Jess, AND GRANNY HAS JUST GIVEN ME MY THIRD GIN & TONIC.

ARE YOU JOKING OR ARE YOU DELIRIOUS? asked her dad.

DELIRIOUS, replied Jess. P.S. WHY DID YOU AND MUM SPLIT UP?

There was a long pause, during which Jess and Granny watched *The Simpsons*, then her dad texted back.

IT'S A LONG STORY, TOO LONG FOR A TEXT. TO DO WITH MY
DREADFUL PERSONALITY DISORDER.

CHICKEN! answered Jess.

I'LL TELL YOU WHEN I SEE YOU, promised her dad. EXCUSE
ME WHILE I VISIT THE N.POLE. ONLY JOKING! GET BETTER SOON.
I LOVE YOU.

Sometime after *The Simpsons*, Jess went to sleep and
dreamt Bart was a real, life-size friend of hers. She was
quite disappointed when she woke up.

Granny pottered about, sat nearby and made her
some dainty little sandwiches, like for a dolls' tea
party. She read Jess extracts from the paper about the
most grisly murders. This passed the time quite
pleasantly until her mum came home. By now Jess's
pains had gone, although she still felt so weak, she
could hardly raise her head. Jess slept again, and
dreamt she was living in a cave in India with an owl.
When she awoke it was 8.30 in the evening. By now
the show would be in full swing. Jess should have
been performing her very first stand-up comedy
routine. Instead she was lying on the sofa, watching a
trashy TV game show.

The next twenty-four hours passed in much the
same way – sleep, lots of drinks and weird dreams.
Halfway through an awful one in which she had three

eyes and grass growing out of her hands, Granny's face appeared in the sky.

'Jess, love,' she said, 'Flora's come to see you. With a boy. I think it might be Fred.'

Jess's grassy hands disappeared and were replaced by the front room. Jess struggled up to a sitting position.

'Shall I bring them in?' asked Granny. 'Are you well enough to see them?' Oh no! The sofa was covered with sweaty bedclothes! Jess's own pyjamas smelt like the zoo! She ran her fingers through her hair – it was a bird's nest. As for her face – well, she hadn't looked in the mirror for more than two whole days. This was a record, but it was also a disaster. What had become of her eyebrows?

'Oh, all right, bring them in,' said Jess.

Granny nipped out again and the next minute Flora came in, not with Fred, but with Ben Jones. Jess felt relieved but also somehow disappointed. They peeped round the door as if they were afraid of what they might see.

'Welcome to my swamp,' croaked Jess. 'Sorry about the stink.'

That was it, then. Ben Jones would never, ever ask her out again, now he had seen her like this.

'You poor thing, Jess!' cried Flora. 'We've brought you some grapes. Don't worry – I've washed them.'

Granny bustled about, found a plate for the grapes, arranged them nicely by Jess's sofa, offered Flora and Ben some juice, and then discreetly went off to her room and shut the door. Flora and Ben sat on the floor, side by side, looking strangely like a pair of twins: both fair, both good-looking, with matching blue eyes. *They're made for each other*, thought Jess. *It's only a matter of time before they realise it. I won't mind. I'll prepare myself.*

'So, how did it go?' croaked Jess.

'Oh, Jess, it was brilliant!' said Flora. 'The whole show was brilliant.'

'What about the band?' asked Jess.

'It was great!' said Flora. 'I couldn't believe it. Everybody was cracking up even before we started to speak or anything – just the way we looked. You're a genius, Jess. It was all your idea.'

'Um, shame you couldn't do your stand-up routine,' said Ben. 'I was really looking forward to seeing you do it.'

'Well, some other time, I suppose,' said Jess. There was a silence. It became, in some curious but definite way, an awkward silence. Oh-oh. Perhaps Ben and

Flora had started going out already. Perhaps they had walked here hand-in-hand. Perhaps they had shared a kiss beneath the bus shelter to nerve themselves up for the ordeal of telling Jess.

'Is something wrong?' asked Jess. It was a bit much having to take the initiative while actually ill, but somebody had to. *Go on, go on*, thought Jess. *Give it to me straight*.

Flora hesitated and blushed. She looked down at the floor. A big, soft, shiny wave of hair fell down across her face. With a gracious, elegant gesture she looped it back round behind her ear. Jess began to write the script for her.

It's like this . . . stammered Flora in Jess's imagination. *Ben and I – well, we've realised that, well, how can I put it? We have become An Item.*

Well, congratulations! replied Jess. She was much better dressed in her fantasy version of things, and her hair, instead of being matted and smelly, shone darkly. And her nose was not at all red and, miraculously, no longer shaped like a cheeky young turnip.

'It's a bit awkward, actually,' began Flora, in real life. 'I'm really, really sorry, Jess – it wasn't my fault.'

Here we go then, thought Jess, and she prepared to

deliver her gracious congratulations. Flora went red again, looked at the floor and fidgeted.

'I didn't feel I could refuse, because Mr Fothergill asked me – he asked me to do your monologue. He'd got a copy, and he said it was a pity that you couldn't do it, so he asked me to do it instead.'

A huge hole seemed to open up in the earth, and Jess felt herself falling down it.

'You – performed my stand-up routine – in the show?' asked Jess faintly. This was not the horrible shock she had been expecting. It was, somehow, ten times worse.

'I'm so sorry, Jess,' said Flora. 'Mr Fothergill introduced it, and he said how sad it was that you were ill and couldn't be there, but he thought your monologue was so good it was a pity to miss out altogether, so he'd asked me to read it.'

'Everybody cracked up,' said Ben. 'It was fantastic. Then at the end they all clapped like mad, and Fothergill said, "Let's have a special round of applause for Jess, and hope she gets better soon," – and the whole school, like, *cheered*, yeah?'

Jess managed somehow to look pleased, and to carry on talking, eventually, about other things. But it was almost like having an out-of-body experience. She could hear herself talking about everyday, unimportant things, but her real self was somewhere else.

The thought of Flora doing her stand-up routine was just absolute torture. And it made it worse that the feeling was kind of selfish and Jess felt ashamed of herself. It was all her own work, and though she had really loved writing it, she had been looking forward to getting up on the stage and performing it to a live audience, more than she had ever looked forward to anything. She hated Flora for having stolen it. She couldn't help it. She knew it wasn't Flora's fault. Mr Fothergill had asked her to do it. But Jess simply hated her.

About half an hour later, Jess's voice gave out and she started coughing. Granny came back in and said they should let her get some rest.

'Don't kiss me goodbye,' said Jess to Flora. 'I might be infectious.'

Then, at last, they were gone.

'What nice young people,' said Granny. 'How sweet of them to come and cheer you up, love.'

Jess nodded. She didn't feel they'd come to cheer her up. She felt as if she'd been mugged. She pulled the blanket over her head and, in the half-dark, stared at the one face who would never disappoint or betray her – the one face that would be with her for the whole of her life, and never, ever change. Her teddy bear Rasputin.

'Watch out, Rasputin,' she whispered. 'I might have to have a bit of a cry in a minute.'

Chapter 27

The next week, Jess went back to school. The first person she met was Jodie, who was standing by the gate reading a newspaper.

'Hey, you're back!' cried Jodie. 'Great! It's such a shame you missed the show! Look – the newspaper's out!'

Jess saw the headline:

FLORA BARCLAY STEALS THE SHOW

'Steals' was right. Jess's eyes tore through the account of the show, written by 'Cruella de Vile' – Fred's alias, of course.

Flora Barclay triumphed in the school show last week, not only fronting the hilarious cod band Poisonous Trash, *but*

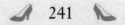

241

stepping in to rescue her best friend, Jess Jordan's, stand-up routine when Jess fell ill and was unable to appear.

There followed a detailed description of Flora's wit, poise and comic energy, ending up predicting a brilliant career for her '*on TV, or possibly in Hollywood*'. Jess felt sick. She really ought not to resent this so much, but she simply couldn't help it. She felt as if her insides were full of black tar.

'My eco-piece is on page seven,' said Jodie. 'But please don't read it because it is *so* dull.'

'I'll go and buy my own copy!' said Jess. 'My mum will want to read it, too, cos she's an eco-warrior!' And she walked swiftly into school, dreading seeing everybody, even the people she was most fond of.

All morning, Flora was in a kind of haze of joy. She was trying very hard to be normal, but everybody was coming up to her and saying, 'Hey! You made it! You're the star of the school!' Everyone was licking her shoes and begging her to carve her autograph in their bare flesh with her nail scissors. Or that's how it seemed to Jess. 'Oh, hi, Jess,' they'd say afterwards. If they noticed her at all. When the bell rang for the lunch break, Jess just wanted to get away. She racked her brains for an excuse to walk off and be by herself. But as it turned out, she didn't need one.

'Jess?' said Flora, looking awkward. 'I need to go and talk something over with Mackenzie. Do you mind? I'm sorry – I'll talk to you later – but this is quite important, OK?'

Jess nodded. Good. She wanted solitude. Flora walked off fast towards the gym, and Jess went off to the furthest corner of the school field and sat down under a tree. She kept tearing the grass up by the handful and throwing it about. But she couldn't seem to uproot the awful feelings that were still planted in her insides.

She and Flora had always been best friends. They had made plans to go to college together, to move to New York and share an apartment, to have glamorous holidays and amazing high-powered jobs in the media. But Jess was beginning to feel that she would always be the hanger-on, the dull, dowdy 'best friend' who comes along to recording sessions and looks after the star's handbag while she dazzles in front of the cameras.

'Hey! So this is where you are!'

A shadow fell across the grass. It was Ben Jones. Jess looked up. The sun was behind his head. She couldn't see his face clearly, but his hair looked like a halo of fire.

'Um – mind if I join you?' he asked.

'Course not,' said Jess.

Ben sat down. There was a silence. He certainly wasn't one of Nature's conversationalists. But at the moment, unusually, neither was Jess.

'Do you know where Flora is?' he asked.

There he goes again, thought Jess. *Obsessed by her. Probably crazy about her. Nothing I can do about it.*

She shrugged. 'She said there was something she had to discuss with Mackenzie.'

'Oh,' said Ben. He looked as if something was troubling him. 'They've been having quite a lot of, like, rows,' he said eventually. 'She seems really sort of irritated with him. Mind you, he is irritating, so possibly that's why.'

Jess sighed. She could see it all. Maybe Ben could sense it, too. Flora was getting tired of Mackenzie. She was beginning to fall for Ben. Ben obviously felt the same about Flora – looking for her, asking about her all the time. But of course it would be awkward for Ben if Flora finished with Mackenzie because of him.

'Can we talk about something else?' asked Jess. 'I'm kind of bored with all this.'

'So am I,' said Ben.

But Jess knew he wasn't really. They talked about the

latest movies. But Ben never suggested they should go and see one together. Oh no, he was never going to ask her out on a date. That was obvious. She was the dark ugly one who held the star's handbag. He was talking to her to pass the time until his next glimpse of the goddess.

So what, thought Jess. *Good luck to them. I just wish they'd get on with it*. She felt completely prepared. So when she saw Flora coming towards them, up the path and across the grass, Jess felt that she could have written the whole script. It was so freaking predictable.

When Flora got near, Jess could tell that she'd been crying. Ben scrambled to his feet. *Typical male*, thought Jess. *The first sign of emotion and they're off*. Flora arrived. Her eyes were wild. Tears sparkled in her golden eyelashes. Her whole body was trembling.

'I've split up with Mackenzie!' she announced.

Ben sort of flinched, and backed off. 'Oh. Right,' he muttered. 'I'd better . . . See you.' And he walked off, leaving the stage clear for the girls' tête-à-tête.

Obviously he had to withdraw for Flora to have her heart-to-heart with her best mate. A decent distance must be observed. But he must know, now, that his time had come. It was going to be tough for him, with Mackenzie. But it was going to be wonderful for him, with Flora.

Flora watched him walk off. She blew her nose and composed herself.

'It was really awful with Mackenzie,' she said. 'We had the worst scene. He's such a control freak. Just like my dad. He's been trying to dominate me ever since we started going out. And he's so, like, jealous and ambitious. He was really really gutted about what it said in the paper. Like I got the headline and stuff. And he said the band was his idea.'

'Oh well,' said Jess. 'Men! Who needs 'em? Just macho, pathetic, massive egos. Throwing their weight about. Waging war. Beating people up. You're better off without him.'

Flora was silent for a moment.

'Yeah,' she agreed. But there was certainly more on her mind. 'Look, Jess, this is difficult,' she faltered a bit, and also started pulling up handfuls of grass and throwing them about. Pretty soon this part of the school field would be completely bald with emotional trauma.

'What?' asked Jess, though she knew full well what was coming.

'It's not just that Mackenzie wasn't right for me,' said Flora. 'Although obviously that was the main thing. But I – the trouble is, I'm crazy about somebody else.'

Yeah, yeah, thought Jess. 'Oh?' she said. 'Who?'

Flora hesitated. Whole handfuls of grass went flying into the air.

'I'm really sorry, because I know he's always been so special to you,' she stammered. 'But I really can't help what I feel, Jess. I've been trying and trying not to feel this way but it's impossible. The more I try to stifle it, the more intense it gets.'

'Don't worry,' said Jess. 'I've seen this coming for ages.'

'Have you really?' asked Flora, wide-eyed with amazement.

'Oh, yes,' said Jess. 'It was obvious right from the start that Ben wasn't interested in me. I hope you'll both be very happy.'

Flora's mouth dropped open.

There you are, thought Jess. *She's speechless. She's dumbstruck by my insight and my gracious generosity.*

'But, Jess,' said Flora, a huge blush unfolding across her face. 'It's not Ben I'm crazy about. It's Fred.'

Chapter 28

Jess's world seemed to split apart. Words went peculiar. The word 'Fred', for example, stopped having any meaning. Maybe Flora meant something else – or maybe she had said something else. Perhaps she had said 'Ben' and it had just sounded like 'Fred'.

'Fred?' echoed Jess. The word came out in a tiny squeak.

Flora's eyes swivelled around nervously: she looked at the sky, the grass, the tree trunk, her own knees.

'Yes,' she replied. 'Fred.'

It was impossible for Jess to speak. Flora – and Fred? Utterly weird. Jess's heart was leaping about like a cat in a bag. Flora fancied *Fred*? This was so totally out of order, Jess could not comprehend it. She just stared open-mouthed at Flora, looking, for a moment, rather unfortunately like a codfish. Flora began to twist the rings on her fingers in a jittery kind of way.

'It's not a sudden thing,' she said. 'And it's nothing to do with what he said about me in the newspaper.'

She blushed, and her eyes sparkled, even though they were modestly fixed on the earth. Probably beetles were already looking up and falling in love with her. 'I've always, like, you know, loved the way Fred is so – you know, like, clever and funny. Only I didn't let myself get, well, like, too carried away because you and Fred were kind of close. So I, just, well, sort of stifled my feelings for him.'

Stifled her feelings! Wow! Heroic! Give the girl a medal!

'Anyway,' Flora went on, 'recently you haven't, like, spent so much time with Fred, and since you and Ben seem to be getting it together, I thought you wouldn't, you know, like, mind.'

Mind? *Mind?* Jess considered the word 'mind'. It was such miles away from her feelings, she could hardly remember what it meant.

Jess was aware she had absolutely no right to feel anything. She didn't own Fred. They weren't even on speaking terms these days. But deep inside, she knew that if Flora started going out with Fred, it was war. Jess could eat all the carpets in the world, tear down all the curtains, break all the windows in the country and still come nowhere near to expressing her absolute horror and fury. She was astonished by her own rage. She knew she wasn't entitled to it. But there it was, blazing away inside her like a vindaloo curry with extra chilli sauce.

'Ben and I are not getting it together,' she said coldly. 'I don't know what gave you that idea.'

Flora's big blue eyes got somehow bigger and bluer in doe-like innocent amazement.

'Well, you're always together,' she said. 'Everyone thinks you're going out.'

'But you're my best friend!' exploded Jess. 'If I was going out with somebody I'd tell you – before I told anybody else. I tell you everything, remember? Though it seems you don't feel the same way about me.'

'I only never mentioned it because I didn't want to hurt you!' Flora retorted. 'I realised it might be horrible for you if Fred and I were going out.'

'Well, rest assured on that one.' Jess managed to control her anger, but she was shaking. 'I wish you both every happiness.'

'Why are you giving me such a hard time, then?' complained Flora.

'I just hate it when you don't tell me things,' said Jess, between clenched teeth. That wasn't it, really.

The truth had dawned on Jess, and it was something she must keep from Flora at all costs.

'So you're really, really OK about it? asked Flora eagerly.

Jess nodded. Flora reached out her arms and gave Jess a hug.

'Oh, thanks, thanks so much, Jess, you're such a babe!' she said. 'I've so dreaded talking to you about Fred. He's so clever and witty and I think his nose is really cute. And I love the way his hair kind of flops about all over the place.'

'I hate his hair,' said Jess. 'And I wish he would cut it. I've told him a hundred times, but he won't listen.'

'I suppose he's always, like, busy thinking about ideas and stuff,' said Flora. 'I think he's a comic genius.'

Jess didn't say much more. She was too shocked to talk properly. She had wasted so many hours preparing herself for the idea that Flora was falling for Ben, and now she had to go back to square one and start all over again. Except this felt so very different that she knew she would never get used to it.

'Please help me, Jess,' said Flora.

'How?' asked Jess, dully, from some deep hole in which she seemed to be sitting.

'The thing is . . . you know Fred. He's always been

one of your best mates . . . I was wondering, could you possibly go and talk to him and, well, you know, like, sound him out type thing? Mention my name and see what kind of reaction you get. And if he seems interested, let him know I'm, well – let him know I like him, too.'

Flora ended this speech with another pretty blush. Jess's imagination reeled at the dreadfulness of this errand.

'If you don't really want to do it,' said Flora, 'I was going to ask Jodie.'

'No!' cried Jess. 'I'll do it! I'll go round his house tonight.' At this point they heard the bell ring distantly for the end of the lunch hour.

The rest of the afternoon passed in a blur. Jess's mind felt like a butterfly against a window pane – fluttering desperately at an invisible barrier, doomed never to escape.

She left school in a daze and started to walk home. Should she go straight round to Fred's or go and see him after supper? Supper, her stomach informed her, was out of the question. This was Jess's own personal Death Row. Maybe she would never eat again. So maybe she should call by straightaway, and get it over with? But what if she nerved herself up to call on her way home, and he wasn't back yet? All that nervous tension for nothing.

'Jess!' She felt a hand on her shoulder. For a brief crazy moment she thought it was Fred. But it was Ben.

'How's Mackenzie?' she asked.

'Gutted,' said Ben, shaking his head and shrugging. 'He's, like, "I'd do anything, anything, to keep her." I told him not to be so stupid. She's never going to change her mind now – is she?'

'No,' sighed Jess. 'I don't think so. I don't know whether she said anything about this to Mackenzie, but she's obsessed with somebody else.'

'No, I don't think she did say that.' Ben frowned. 'Um – who?'

Jess laughed bitterly. 'Ironically, I thought it was going to be you. I know you're interested in her and I don't blame you.'

Ben stood stock-still and stared at Jess in amazement.

'Me?' he gasped. 'Me, interested in Flora?'

'Well, aren't you?' asked Jess.

'No way!' said Ben, grinning in complete shock.

'But you always seemed to want to talk about her – asking me stuff about her all the time.'

'I was just, like, worried about what Mackenzie was

getting himself into,' explained Ben. 'He's one crazy guy, you know. He's got a wild streak. He needs somebody keeping an eye on him. I'm not, like, interested in Flora. No way.'

For a moment Jess thought he was going to confess that he was interested in somebody else. The way he paused, and looked sideways at her, made her panic a bit for a second. Just a few weeks ago, she had often fantasised about Ben Jones walking her home and declaring his undying passion for her. Now the thought scared her to death.

'I'm not interested in any girls, yeah?' said Ben quietly. 'Not in that way. I don't want a girlfriend. I couldn't, like, cope with it.'

Relief surged through Jess.

'Good,' she said. 'I'd hate it if she'd managed to break your heart as well as Mackenzie's.'

'No girl's ever going to break my heart,' Ben assured her. 'Other stuff is so more important.'

'Yeah,' agreed Jess. But right now, she couldn't think of anything.

'So who's the, like, lucky guy?' asked Ben. 'The one Flora's got her eye on?'

'Fred,' said Jess.

'You're kidding!' exclaimed Ben. 'No way! She

shouldn't even go there! So tight! Harsh! Unfair to you!'

'To me?' faltered Jess. She had always thought Ben was a nice guy, but a bit dumb. Now it seemed he was more perceptive – well, more perceptive than Jess herself, on this subject at least.

'But you and Fred are so, like, made for each other,' puzzled Ben. 'Well, aren't you?'

'I don't think so, somehow,' said Jess. 'We're not even speaking at the moment. And once Flora makes a play for anybody – that tends to be it.'

'So has Fred, like, y'know . . . got feelings for Flora?' asked Ben, with a doubtful frown.

Jess sighed. 'Who hasn't? – Apart from you.'

'So they haven't actually, like, got together yet?' asked Ben.

'No,' said Jess. 'Tonight I have the delightful task of going round to his house and broaching the subject.'

'Oh wow!' breathed Ben. 'So harsh! You poor thing!' They had arrived at the road where Ben turned off. 'Good luck, then,' he said, and put his arm briefly round her shoulders. 'Ring me if you want to talk. You know – afterwards, yeah?'

As Jess walked off down the street that led to Fred's house, it did cross her mind briefly that Ben might possibly be gay. She hoped so. It would be so cool. She had always wanted a gay best friend. But somehow she had always assumed it would be Fred.

Fred was turning out to be something else entirely. And in five minutes' time she would be with him. Face to Face. For the showdown.

Chapter 29

Jess arrived at Fred's house and stood on the pavement outside, her heart hammering. Should she call now? Or come back in an hour or two? His mum's car wasn't there, and Jess knew his dad usually came home much later than this. Get it over with. That was best. If she rang first, somehow he might make an excuse and avoid seeing her. She walked up the path and rang the bell.

The door opened and Fred appeared. When he saw her, his face sort of crumpled with dismay.

'This won't take long,' said Jess.

Evidently her presence was odious to him.

'What is it?' asked Fred. 'Assassination? Go ahead. I deserve it.'

'Don't be an idiot,' said Jess. 'I only want a word.'

'A word?' said Fred. 'How about antidisestablish-mentarianism? It's very popular these days. Though personally I find it a bit over the top.'

'Stop trying to make me laugh. I'm not in the mood,' snapped Jess. 'This is serious. Are your parents in?'

'My mum has gone off to groom her racehorses,' said Fred. 'And my dad is helping the police with their enquiries into his money-laundering in Panama.'

'Ask me in, then, why don't you?' grumbled Jess, barging past Fred and going into the sitting room where Fred had so recently spent the night in a sleeping bag, watching violent movies and then sleeping like a baby. That seemed light years ago now. Jess had so loved it here. She had felt almost like part of the family. Now that would be Flora's privilege.

Fred and Jess sat down on opposing sofas. 'Would you like a drink or something?' asked Fred.

'No thanks,' said Jess. 'And I don't want to watch a violent movie either.'

'Nor do I,' said Fred. 'I've gone off them a bit lately. I prefer arty French movies now, to be honest. With subtitles. That *Amélie* is amazing. I've watched it seven times. She looks a bit like you, in fact.'

Jess hadn't seen *Amélie*, so she didn't know whether this was a compliment or an insult. But it didn't matter anyway. It was disconcerting, being here, with Fred being his old self. Jess longed just to relax into the easy feeling and forget her mission. But she couldn't. She had promised Flora.

There was a silence. Fred was staring at her. Jess was confused for a second, jittery. She was so preoccupied with what she had to say that she wasn't concentrating properly. Had he just asked her something? She stared back. He tossed his hair out of his eyes and gave a tense, nervy smile.

'Sorry,' he said suddenly.

'Sorry for what?' asked Jess.

'I dunno – sorry for everything,' he said. 'I always apologise to everybody whenever I meet them just in case I might have committed a nuisance upon them while engaged in astral travel.'

'I'm the one who should apologise,' said Jess.

'No, I'm the one!' snapped Fred in mock rivalry. 'I'm sorry, OK? I'm sorry. Not you. I'm sorry but there it is – I'm sorry.'

'Well, I'm sorry about ruining your mum's birthday,' said Jess.

'No, it was fine,' said Fred, but he blushed.

'I said I'd been sick,' Jess went on, 'but the truth was I'd had to help my granny. She left the kitchen tap on and the water overflowed all over the ground floor, and I had to look after her and clear it all up, and I didn't realise how late it was getting, and –'

'Forget it,' said Fred. 'My mum had a headache anyway, so we decided to postpone her birthday party until the summer holidays.'

Jess felt immensely relieved to hear this. Maybe she would have a chance to get Fred's mum a present after all – with her own money this time.

'So you're not mad at me?' said Jess.

Fred grinned at her through his locks of hair. 'I thought *you* were mad at *me*,' he said. 'I meant to ask you to write for the newspaper. You were the first person I thought of. I even rang you once, but your granny answered the phone. I was so freaked out by it I thought I'd wait till I saw you at school. But somehow – whenever I got the chance . . .'

'What?' cried Jess. 'What?'

'Well, you know . . .' Fred looked a bit awkward, and began to fiddle with his trainers. 'When someone's going out with someone, one has to keep one's distance.'

'Who?' demanded Jess, fear striking into her heart. 'Who are you going out with?'

Fred looked startled. 'Me?' he asked, in a camp pose with his hand on his chest. '*Moi?* Going out with somebody? Like, who? An alien, perhaps? Or some kind of exotic cabbage plant?'

'Oh, I thought you meant *you* were going out with somebody,' said Jess, feeling rather breathless all of a sudden.

'No, I meant *you*,' explained Fred patiently, as if to a very young child or forgetful old person.

'*Me?*' gasped Jess. '*I'm* not going out with anybody!'

'But,' faltered Fred, 'what about Ben? Everybody says you're going out. I see you everywhere together. Walking home, sitting on the wall, in the library at lunchtime, in the canteen . . . Whizzer said . . . he said Ben was over at your place the day of my mum's birthday thing.'

'That was nothing!' said Jess. 'He just called by to lend me a DVD. I didn't even want to watch the stupid thing. I just didn't want to be rude. He didn't even come indoors.'

'So you're not going out with him?' asked Fred. His eyes were starting to sparkle in a truly festive way.

'Of course we're not going out!' Jess assured him. 'He just talks to me a lot because Mackenzie's always with Flora – I mean, we both had time on our hands.'

'Oh,' said Fred.

Another silence sprang up. This one seemed a bit

more relaxed than the previous silence, and yet a bit more dangerous. Jess scrambled to fill it. She must, she must, deliver her message.

'But things have changed, anyway, because Flora's split up with Mackenzie,' she said.

'Oh well,' said Fred. 'So?'

Jess hesitated. Now she was coming to the breathless moment.

'Flora says it's not fair on Mackenzie to be going out with him, because she really wants to go out with somebody else.'

Fred shrugged and pulled an ape-face.

'The thing is, Fred . . . she wants to go out with you.'

Fred kind of leapt back on the sofa as if he'd been shot. His eyes were huge with amazement. For once, he could not say anything. He just stared at Jess, open-mouthed.

'Yeah,' Jess went on. 'Apparently she's been crazy about you for some time. She thinks you're a comic genius.'

Fred shook his head, then rubbed his face, then scowled at the carpet, then shook his head again.

'No,' he said. 'No . . . no . . . no . . . no! It's absurd. I don't want to go out with a girl who thinks I'm a comic genius. I'd rather go out with a girl . . .' He peeped at Jess through his locks of floppy hair. 'I'd rather go out with a girl who thinks I'm an owl. I mean, swooping about at night and ripping the heads off small rodents – that's achievable.'

Jess's heart did that hurtling-out-of-her-mouth trick, performed a circuit of Fred's sitting room, bounced off the window and re-entered her body at speed through her bottom. Had Fred said he wanted to go out with her?

'Are you saying . . .' She had to be bold and seize the moment. 'Are you saying you want to go out with me?'

'Yeah, all right then, why not give it a whirl,' said Fred quickly, as if they were discussing whether to have a new sort of sandwich. 'I'm not proposing marriage, mind you. I'm not the marrying kind.'

'Don't worry,' said Jess. 'Nor am I. In fact, I'd rather be marooned in the Gobi desert and groomed to death by meerkats than marry you.'

'Couldn't agree more,' said Fred. 'I'd rather be deep-fried in egg and breadcrumbs than be married to you for even a split second.'

'Thank goodness we've got that clear, then,' said Jess.

There was another silence. This time it was just intensely delicious.

'There's something I've been meaning to say to you for some time,' said Fred. His eyes were dancing.

'What?' asked Jess.

'Well . . .' Fred picked up a cushion and hugged it. 'It's kind of hard to say, really . . . it's just, you know: three little words.'

Jess was on her guard. Maybe there was a trick coming. Or maybe this was the happiest moment of her life so far.

'What three little words?' she said. '*You're an idiot?*'

'No,' replied Fred. '*Cut my hair.*'

'Cut your hair?' exclaimed Jess. 'What a brilliant, brilliant idea! I've wanted to cut your hair for about a thousand years. But we'll have to wash it first.'

They went up to the bathroom together and surveyed Fred's mum's immense range of desirable shampoos.

'What sort of hair have you got?' demanded Jess.

'Hair that hasn't been washed for decades,' replied Fred. He sat down on the bathroom stool. 'Have a look,' he invited her.

Jess touched his hair. It was soft and clean. It had so clearly been washed yesterday. But she didn't say a word. It was just great to be doing this.

'I recommend your mum's coconut and cinnamon shampoo,' she said.

'Go on, then,' said Fred. 'Wash it.' And he stuck his head over the washbasin. 'Our shower head's broken,' he mumbled. 'You'll have to use a glass.'

Jess made sure the water was just right: warm, not hot. Ever so gently, she wet his hair. Then she applied the shampoo and massaged it in. Then she rinsed it, stroking the streams of warm water out of Fred's long floppy locks. It took ages, just using the glass. Halfway through the rinsing, Fred put his arm round her waist.

'I'm frightened of water,' he said. 'You'll have to excuse me.'

At last Jess had finished, and they went downstairs. Fred had a towel round his shoulders like a tennis player.

'I'd better cut it in your utility room,' said Jess. 'Where you've got those ceramic tiles. If we did it in here, the hair would stick to the carpet.'

'That's what I love about you,' said Fred. 'You're so sensible.'

They went into the utility room. Fred sat down. Jess found some scissors in the kitchen, and propped a large mirror against the wall, on top of the washing machine.

'So how do you want it?' she asked.

'Whatever you like,' said Fred cheerfully. 'I'm sick of the stuff. The shorter the better.'

Jess had never cut anybody's hair before, but it seemed easy. A lot of hair fell on the floor. Fred's head emerged. It looked crisp and cool. Better defined. So completely and utterly Fred. It was as if all the irritating things about Fred had dropped away on to the floor, as well as the hair. And all the bad times they'd had, also.

'You know what hairdressers always say?' said Jess. '*Going anywhere nice for your holiday?*' She put on a camp hairdresser's voice.

'Well, I was torn between Ibiza and Berlin,' said Fred. 'But I suppose we could have quite a good time down the road, in the park.'

A glorious summer in the park with Fred began to shimmer in Jess's imagination.

'I'd really like to write some comedy with you,' he went on. 'That stand-up of yours was the funniest thing ever. Do it for me now – go on!'

'Certainly not!' said Jess playfully. 'Things have moved on in the Lonely Hearts department. That stand-up routine is So Last Season.'

'OK, then,' said Fred. 'But could we write some stuff for, like, a double act? You and me?'

266

'Yeah,' said Jess. 'We could create a couple of old codgers called Doris and Arthur. You could play Doris and I could play Arthur.'

'We could even go somewhere on a trip,' mused Fred.

'Yeah!' said Jess. 'We could go and see my dad down in St Ives! And my other project for the summer is, I've really got to find out why my mum and dad split up.'

'I've really got to find out why my mum and dad *didn't*,' sighed Fred.

The haircut was finished.

'Wow!' said Jess. 'You look a bit like a bushbaby! Can I stroke your head?'

'Please,' said Fred. 'Be my guest.'

Jess stroked it. It did feel a bit like the fur of an animal.

'I shall start purring in a minute,' said Fred. 'You can stroke my head any time you like. In fact, I shall get rather annoyed if you don't stroke it every day.'

Jess, standing behind Fred, put her arms round his shoulders. Fred reached up and held her hands in close to his heart. Jess could feel it racing. She rested her head on top of his head. They looked at themselves in the mirror.

'What an ugly couple,' said Fred.

They stayed like that for quite a while, just grinning at each other in the mirror. All around them, on the floor, Fred's hair shone in the sunlight. It was going to be one terrific summer.

Hi, guys!

You're so brilliant reading this and it's really cheered me up, as Fred is being a bit of a toad at the moment — not that he's covered with warts and is shooting poison out of his neck (but give him time). Sometimes I feel that you're my only friend, especially when Flora's at orchestra practice. So please, please, do me a ginormous favour and visit my fabulous, dazzling, low-calorie, high-energy website — www.JessJordan.co.uk!!!!

I'm going to be blogging away (I wrote *glogging* by accident at first and I kind of like it, so I might be glogging too) and I can promise you loads of laughs, polls, quizzes, interactive stuff, downloadable goodies, plus sensational secrets that Fred, Flora, Ben, Mackenzie and Jodie have begged me to never reveal! Don't tell them I sent you — and promise you'll be there!

Love,
Jess!

Jess's Hilarious Recipe for a Mouth-watering Comedy Routine

Select a piece of paper, preferably not one previously used for wrapping chips.

Select a pen.

Avoid computers — you could end up surfing for shoes. (You know it's true!)

Create a character who is like you, but worse — or, in my case, even worse.

Chew your pen, dipped in ketchup if you like it.

Give your character something they must do e.g. complete already-late homework, organise a birthday present for their mum or walk the neighbour's dog.

Arrange interruptions e.g. an explosion of ancient yogurt, a text message from their mate reporting a fight in the park, the delivery of a mysterious parcel or the appearance of a bold, taunting cat.

Stir, simmer for ten minutes, scatter with jokes 'n' quips then serve immediately.

For more top tips from Jess, visit www.JessJordan.co.uk

Loved this story about Jess?

You'll adore

Absolute Torture!

Chapter 1

Disaster! Jess tried to hide her horror.

Her mum frowned. 'What's wrong, sweetheart? It's what you've always wanted. A trip to see your dad! I rang him about it last night and he can't wait to see you! And there'll be sun, sea, art and ice cream! Plus lots of interesting places on the way down to Cornwall. It's the holiday of a lifetime. For goodness' sake, Jess! What's the matter?'

Jess could not possibly, ever, tell. She would rather run through the supermarket stark naked and farting than reveal her secret to Mum. This sudden fabulous surprise holiday was going to ruin her life, big time. Jess's heart sank and sank and sank until it was right down on the carpet like a very ill pet.

But she must try and sound delighted. 'Nothing's wrong! I've just got a bit of a headache. But hey, Mum!

Thanks! It'll be fantastic! When do we leave?' She tried desperately to force a bit of enthusiasm into her voice, but it was hopeless – like trying to cram her bum into size 10 jeans.

'We'll set off the day after tomorrow,' said her mum, with the excited smile of a practised torturer. 'Early. There won't be so much traffic then, and we can just potter gently down into the countryside. Oh, I can't wait! It's going to be marvellous!'

Mum's eyes glazed over and she stared out of the window with a look of faraway rapture, as if the angel of the Lord had just appeared over Tesco's.

'Ruined abbeys!' she drooled. 'Rare wild flowers! Bronze Age burial mounds!'

Jess sometimes thought her mum was slightly off her head. Maybe if her parents had stayed together it would have kept Mum sane. But then again, maybe not. Her dad was kind of crazy, too.

'Start packing!' said Mum. 'You've only got twenty-four hours!' And she rushed off upstairs, possibly to pack *Fabulous Fossils and Fascinating Cracks in the Ground* or *Stylish Sea Urchins of the South West*.

Twenty-four hours! Jess had to think fast. She had just one day to put an end to this horrendous talk of a holiday. Could she become dangerously ill in twenty-four hours? Could she discreetly vandalise the car so it would never, ever, start again? Could she, acting with utmost care of course, slightly burn the house down?

She had to see Fred. Dear Fred! He would know what to do. Perhaps they could elope. Although they had no money. Perhaps they could elope to the bottom of his garden. It was a bit overgrown down there. There was a huge tree. They could secretly live in the tree. A bit like Tarzan and Jane, only without the muscles or the beauty.

Darling Fred! She had to text him now! Jess raced up to her bedroom but – how cruel fate was – her mobile phone had disappeared. The floor of her room was covered with scattered heaps of clothes, CDs, books and empty chocolate wrappers, as if it had been ransacked by wild animals in the night. Jess flung the debris around for a moment and then decided to cut her losses and just go round to Fred's house without texting him. He was bound to be there. He almost never went anywhere without telling her these days.

She just had to check her make-up first. Jess headed for the kitchen where there was a small mirror above the sink, so you could stare into your own tortured eyes as you washed the dishes. She sighed. Her eyebrows were rubbish. They would have been rubbish even on an orang-utan.

Never mind. This was no time to pluck an eyebrow. She flung open the fridge and grabbed a can of Coke. No, wait, that should be water. Although she and Fred were close, they hadn't yet passed the gas barrier. Silent pants were desirable in his company.

Jess got a glass of water and drank it while looking in the mirror. *Glug, glug, glug* went her throat, like a snake eating a whole family of gerbils. Most unattractive.

'Have you seen my teeth?' came a sudden spooky voice behind her. But it wasn't a spectral presence. It was only Granny. Actually, what she said was, 'Have you feen my teeth?' because when she lost her teeth she couldn't pronounce her 's's. She called Jess 'Jeff'. This was slightly irritating. Jess wasn't completely opposed to the idea of a sex change, but if she did unexpectedly become a male person, she wanted to be called Justin, not Jeff.

'Have you looked under your pillow?' asked Jess. They went into Granny's room and found the teeth immediately.

'My goodneff, you are brilliant at finding things, dear,' said Granny. 'You fould work in airport fecurity when you leave fchool.'

Jess laughed. Granny's teeth were always either in a glass of water on the bedside table, or under the pillow.

'No, Granny, I'm going to be a stand-up comedian, remember?' said Jess. 'Not as glamorous as airport security, obviously, but somebody's got to perform the back-breaking drudgery of making people laugh.'

Granny picked up her teeth and for a moment used them in a kind of ventriloquist act.

'Hello, Jeff!' she said in a squeaky voice she always used for the teeth. 'What'f for fupper?' Granny made the teeth chomp together in a hungry kind of way.

This little cabaret had amused Jess quite a lot when she was younger, but now, quite frankly, it was beginning to lose its allure. Jess was desperate to escape and fly to the arms of Fabulous Fred. She laughed politely and backed off down the hallway towards the front door.

'Let'f go and watch the news,' said Granny, ramming her teeth back into her mouth with panache. 'There's been an explosion in Poland, it's terrible. Hundreds feared dead.' Granny was quite ghoulish in her addiction to catastrophe.

'I've got to go out, Granny,' said Jess, looking at her watch in an important way. 'I've got to say goodbye to my friends before I go on holiday.'

'Ah! Our lovely trip! I'm so looking forward to it, dear, aren't you? Grandpa and I spent our honeymoon in Cornwall, you know.'

Jess had heard this story approximately 99,999 times. *Please don't say anything more about it, Granny*, she thought desperately, *or I might just have to bundle you away affectionately but briskly into the cupboard under the stairs*.

'And,' Granny went on excitedly, 'I'm taking Grandpa's ashes so I can throw them into the sea!'

Jess smiled through gritted teeth and reached behind her to open the front door.

'Lovely, Granny! Fabulous idea! Ashes, sea – go for it! Kind of like the afterlife is a scuba-diving holiday!'

Granny laughed. She was amazingly broad-minded and would probably laugh at her own funeral.

'Now you must excuse me, Granny – I really must go! Flora's waiting for me in the park!'

'Oh, all right dear – I'll keep you posted on the Polish explosion when you get back!' promised Granny.

She trotted eagerly into the sitting room, heading for the TV. It was already two minutes past five and she might have missed some glorious brand-new disaster. Granny had come to live with them fairly recently and it had certainly brightened things up in the Jordan household. However, right now Jess's thoughts were elsewhere.

She ran out of the house and sped down the road. It had been a lie about Flora waiting for her in the park. An excuse to get away. The person she really had to see was Fred.

Please God, she prayed as she hurtled off towards the sacred house where the divine Fred Parsons lived. *Save me, please, from this terrible holiday! Sprain my ankle! Sprain both my ankles! And please let Fred be in!*

Chapter 2

As she ran to Fred's house, Jess tried to get a grip on the situation. But it was totally out of control. The best summer ever had turned into howling darkness in less than half an hour.

Jess and Fred had only just become an item, and they had planned to spend the whole summer together in the park. They were going to have a picnic lunch under a different tree every day. They had even planned some bus trips out of town, to wander through forests or walk hand in hand on a beach, 'like an insurance ad', as Fred had put it.

And of course, once it got dark, they would probably have spent hours and hours practising the tiresome business of kissing and cuddling. Every night for the past week, by the park gates, in a private dark place under a tree, Fred had kissed her goodnight. Jess's skin sort of sizzled at the memory of it.

'I suppose we'd better go through the whole meaningless charade of a goodnight kiss – if we can manage it,' Fred had murmured the first time. 'In fact, I've been chewing gum all evening in preparation for this moment.' He had spat out his gum – quite stylishly into a rubbish bin – and they had gone for it.

Their first kiss. It had been long, slow and delicious. Jess's heart had gone into overdrive. And eventually, when they pulled apart, Fred had whispered, 'What do you think of that? Awful, wasn't it?'

'Nauseating!' Jess had sighed, and laid her head on his heart.

What fatal instinct had made her mum choose this moment to plan a holiday? The very moment when suddenly just being at home had become heaven on earth? Normally, of course, Jess would have loved nothing more than to go down to the seaside and visit her slightly crazy but totally cute dad, and help him with his rather gloomy paintings of beaches and seagulls. But just right now . . . the thought of going away was torture.

It was impossible to tell her mum, hopeless to try and explain. If Jess even tried she would be in the worst trouble ever. Because Jess's mum wasn't what you'd call boy-friendly. She wasn't a man-hater exactly, but she only ever let men into the house if the washing machine wasn't working.

Jess sometimes thought she would never have the courage to defy her mum's disapproval and get married. She would have to go and live thousands of miles away in Kalamazoo and pretend her husband was a large dog called Henry.

Jess arrived at Fred's house, panting. She had run all the way. *If you want to get fit*, she thought, *don't join a gym – fall in love*. She rang the doorbell and tried to put on a casual, glamorous expression, even though her cheeks were bright red and her lungs were wheezing like an old church organ infested with termites.

Fred's father opened the door. Behind him, Jess could hear football on TV.

'Is Fred in?' she panted.

Fred's dad shook his head.

'He's gone out,' he said.

'Oh no! Do you know where he's gone?' cried Jess in dismay.

Fred's dad shrugged.

'Sorry,' he said in a final kind of way. He didn't invite Jess in to wait till Fred got back. Fred's mum would have known what to do. She would have invited Jess in, offered delicious food and drink, and settled her down to wait with albums full of adorable photos of the infant Fred.

But his dad was a complete duffer.

'Excuse me,' he said now, as the sound of the football crowd soared in excitement on the TV, 'I must get back to the football.' And, with a regretful smile, he shut the door in her face.

Jess was devastated, paralysed and appalled. Fred's whole street seemed to go dark. Black clouds were gathering, and she had a feeling that vultures were circling overhead. For a moment she was on the verge of tears, but she managed to get rid of them by sort of swallowing the back of her nose. It tasted vile. What should she do now? Where should she go? She was facing disaster, and where was Fred when she needed him? Mysteriously and infuriatingly out.

She only had one hope. She had to go and see her best friend Flora. Thank goodness Flora hadn't gone on holiday yet. She was due to leave in a couple of days on a 'Costa Rican Adventure'. Jess wasn't sure exactly where Costa Rica was, but the photos in the brochure suggested that Flora would be trekking through rainforests full of beautiful birds and butterflies and relaxing on tropical beaches under swaying palm trees.

Flora's family could afford such treats because her dad was very big in bathrooms. But this time Jess hadn't felt jealous of Flora's holiday at all, because nothing in the world could be better than just hanging out in the park, all summer, with Fred.

There had been a slightly dodgy moment a few weeks ago, before Jess and Fred had got together, when Flora had revealed that she was crazy about Fred. But once Fred had confessed his perverted preference for dark, imperfect Jess rather than blonde, perfect Flora, Flora had dug deep into her character and produced an unsuspected angelic streak. She had only sulked about it for three days.

Jess broke into a run. She desperately needed some sympathy and Flora was usually very prompt with the hugs and hot chocolate.

The front door was opened by Flora's older sister, Freya. Freya was at Oxford, studying maths. Like all Flora's family, she was blonde and almost illegally beautiful. She was kind of vague and dreamy as well, which somehow added to her angelic charm. If Jess had tried to be vague and dreamy it wouldn't have worked. She would just have appeared overweight and idiotic.

'Oh – er – hello, Jess . . .' murmured Freya. 'Flora's . . . where is Flora? Er, yes, um, I think she's in the sitting room with Mummy . . .' And she drifted off to do some very hard sums or possibly rinse her hair in extract of camomile flowers. Jess took off her shoes (one always had to do this at Flora's because of the blonde carpets) and tiptoed to the sitting room. How soon would she be able to get Flora on her own and cry on her shoulder?

But an amazing sight met Jess's startled gaze. Flora's mother, who on a good day could pass for a minor movie star, was lying on the sofa with a badly bruised cheekbone and a black eye, and with her leg in plaster! What on earth had happened? It seemed that Jess would be expected to provide sympathy instead of receiving it. How unfair life was!

Get to Know Sue Limb with her Q & A!

🌸 **Name:** Sue Limb.

🌸 **Star sign:** Virgo.

🌸 **Favourite colour:** Green.

🌸 **Favourite number:** Seven.

🌸 **Favourite thing to do:** Give my dog a bath.

🌸 **Favourite food:** Anything with pesto.

🌸 **Where were you born?** Hitchin, Hertfordshire, England.

✸ **Where do you live now?** On a remote farm in Gloucestershire.

✸ **What were you like at school?** A tomboy-ish nerd.

✸ **Have you got brothers and sisters?** One older brother, who's a jazz musician.

✸ **What did you want to be as a child?** Secretary-General of the United Nations (I told you I was a nerd).

✸ **How did you start writing?** At age two, I liked doodling the letter 'S'. When I grew up, I tried teaching, couldn't cope, and writing seemed to be the only thing possible.

✸ **What did you do before you were a writer?** I was a teacher, screaming in vain for quiet while my classes rioted gently around me.

✸ **Where do you write?** Anywhere – I particularly like writing on trains. But when I'm at home, in a room with windows opening into a wild wood.

* **What was your favourite book as a child?** *The Railway Children* by E. Nesbit.

* **What's your favourite children's book now?** *Where the Wild Things Are* by Maurice Sendak.

* **What's your favourite adult book?** *Persuasion* by Jane Austen.

* **What tips do you have for budding writers?** Read a lot!

* **What's your favourite TV programme?** *Frasier*.

* **What makes you laugh?** Harry Enfield and Paul Whitehouse as the Surgeons.

* **What's your favourite movie?** *Some Like It Hot*.

* **Who do you imagine playing Jess, Flora and Fred in a movie?** Carey Mulligan would be Jess, Emma Watson would be Flora and Jamie Campbell Bower would be Fred.